新制多益

聽力題庫

會話大全❷（附詳盡解析）

TOEIC

Amanda
Chou ◎ 著

四大特色

1 **影子跟讀設計：聽力專注力和理解力猛提升**
收錄海量對話練習，反覆聽誦與跟讀，潛移默化提升聽力「專注力」和「理解力」，無形中累積高分實力。

2 **新制題型強化：臨危不亂地應對所有考題**
有效補強考生答三人以上的對話、慣用語題型的答題能力，穩收高分成效。

3 **職場主題連結：畢業即就業**
將考試主題與職場情境結合，步入職場後能迅速融入工作岡位，工作上更為如虎添翼。

4 **核心能力提升：推測和理解等關鍵聽力能力的掌握**
側重核心能力的養成，考點融會貫通後，即迅速拆解「推測」、「暗示性」等題型，難題均能迎刃而解。

MP3

作者序

　　在新多益聽力測驗，英文會話的題目佔了總題數的39%，卻影響著大多數初、中階備考考生欲達到求職的新多益門檻，即550-750這個區間的分數。這也意謂有著紮實的會話題的練習、多樣化的主題和更貼近生活和職場的會話內容，對考生來說是必須的。

　　然而，聽力高分也並非一蹴可幾，在《**新制多益聽力題庫：會話大全(1)**》的出版後，甫即規劃了《**會話大全(2)**》，當中涵蓋了不重疊的對話主題，讓考生有更廣泛的練習題材，且能循序漸進地累積聽力實力。這兩本均適合初期備考，且在規劃上降低了考生的挫折感，由單一會話題逐步朝向一整組的完整會話模擬試題練習。考生先藉由包羅萬象的會話題中一篇篇的掌握當中的相關字彙和慣用語、答題技巧等，最後在適應答一整組的會話模擬試題（即13篇會話題組）。這當中分拆掉了要許多初、中階考生一次要寫完100題完整模擬試題的難度。（大多數高中生、大學生的英文程度大約落在450-750這個區間，而在具備新多益總分750的考生才比較適合直接大量撰寫新多益題庫以提升聽、讀的答題能力。）

如果有考過官方多益測驗，但卻未達到某個分數段的考生來説。建議可以單獨買會話大全系列，先藉由廣泛的主題練習，將重點著重在「累積聽力能力」而非「達到某個分數段」或是買一整回的題庫猛練（題庫比較適合衝刺分數或應考前密集練習熟悉題型，對於大多數初、中階考生要累積聽力能力是不太相同的。題庫比較像是累積一定英文聽力基礎的考生或是外文系學生，是經過一定大學英文訓練後，應試前買來練習用的）。相信在這些密集的練習和累積後，再去寫一整回模擬試題是較符合大多數學習者的規劃。另外，考生也可以先藉由單獨強化《會話》和《短獨白》，再來寫一整回聽力模擬試題100題，相信會頓時覺得備考壓力輕鬆了許多。

Amanda Chou

使用說明

INSTRUCTIONS

基礎實力養成，完成所有填空題
聽力細節的掌握能力也同步飆升

· 先藉由填空題演練，掌握字彙部分，再延伸學習到聆聽一
  整篇對話，大幅降低挫折感，增進學習動力。
· 掌握必考商業和生活字彙並反覆練習，直至所有規劃的填
  空練習均能聽對，再進行聽一段對話並完成試題的練習。

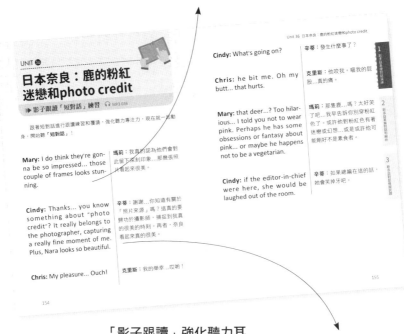

「影子跟讀」強化聽力耳
聽力專注力立馬到位，答題不失分

· 由「中英對照」的對話以影子跟讀法進行練習，從「看原
  稿跟著音檔讀」逐步延伸至「只播放音檔也能同步跟著讀」
  等等的練習，打好聽力專注力基礎。並於具備一定的聽力
  專注力後再輔以海量的試題搭配練習，分數迅速狂飆。

附選項中譯和詳盡解析
徹底理解所有出題脈絡

· 提供更多元的答題思路，逐步協助考生進行推論或刪去誘答選項，釐清頭緒後迅速判答，如同有英文家教在旁的神力加持，自觀自學即可完成所有試題並具備應考判答實力。

place we can't quite figure out.

在我們無法找到的某些地方。

Jason: That rocks!

傑森：棒呆了。

選項中譯與解析

19. 根據對話，"an ugly wall"是指什麼？
(A) 沒刷好又醜的牆
(B) 展示自然風景面的牆壁
(C) 看起來很破舊的牆
(D) 展出人們狀態不佳照的一道牆

20. 為何男子說「這很不恰當」？
(A) 他因被羞辱而感到生氣。
(B) 他不認為羞辱別人感覺會有多好。
(C) 醜陋牆不適合這個活動名稱。
(D) 美貌牆不合適。

21. 談話者接下來可能會做何事？
(A) 把醜陋牆上的照片拿走
(B) 學習如何使用照片編輯裝置
(C) 收集員工看起來美美的照片
(D) 粉刷醜陋牆，如此看起來好多了

19.
· 聽到對話，馬上鎖定 ugly wall和what's that 推測是真正意思。此題屬於推測題，此種推測題，通常在對話中會出現一問一答。考生掌握對話的問題，仔細聽回答，再推測哪個選項描述的意思最接近此答案。考

224

點引用句的另一線索字是photo，四個選項中，只有**選項(D)**...displays photos... 出現。另外一個重點，ugly wall直接翻譯是醜牆，通常答案不會是直翻，會有陷阱。因此，聽到女子問What's that? 男子回答 Putting a bunch of pictures, making fun of someone. 可推測出來。

20.
· 聽到對話，馬上鎖定inappropriate和其後面的對話 Humiliating someone in exchange of...，推測是「不滿，不適合」的意思。此題屬於推測題，也同時測試考生對單字"humiliate"和"mock"的理解。考生必須先懂這個單字的意思，再推測哪個選項描述的意思最接近此意。考點引用句的另一線索字是Humiliating someone，羞辱別人，看到(A)... that he was humiliated... (D) A beauty wall...，刪去(A)&(D)，因為該話者並沒有被羞辱，以及beauty wall和主題不和。再比較(B) & (C)，刪去(C)，因為(C)a proper name... 意思是針對活動名稱，所以(B)He doesn't think it's nice. 「他不認為...好」是最佳選項。

21.
· 聽到對話，馬上鎖定 對話最後的幾句，推測是進行「美貌牆」之事。此題屬於推測題，也同時測試考生對前後語意關聯的理解，考生必須了解幾句話的關聯性，再選出最接近的選項。考點引用句的另一線索字是 do a beauty wall，所以有可能的答案，和此有關。本題有點弔詭，四個選項都和對話有連結。因此，必須有刪去法，選出最適合且最合理的要做。(A) take away the photos on the ugly wall → 這不是接下來要做。(B) learn how to use photo editing APPs→ 文中提到使用，表示已使用。(C) gather employees' photos in which they look good→ 因為美貌牆，必須用美照。(D) paint the ugly wall so that it will look better→ 這跟牆壁本身無關。

225

Unit 7 醜陋牆遠不如美麗牆

1 新多益聽讀對話與演講

2 新多益聽讀對話和對動

3 新多益聽讀解對話

005

演練 **13** 篇為一組的英文對話
適應應考時英文對話節奏

- 習慣性聽此長度的英文對話，立即熟悉一整回聽力模擬試題中對話練習量（即 13 篇），漸進式養成具備獨立撰寫聽力試題的實力。
- 搭配所附的中英對照和解析，雙重檢視學習成果，一舉攻略新多益聽力。

聽力模擬試題

▶ **PART 3** MP3 059

Directions: In this part, you will listen to several conversations between two or more speakers. These conversations will not be printed and will only be spoken one time. For each conversation, you will be asked to answer three questions. Select the best response and mark the corresponding letter (A), (B), (C), (D) on the answer sheet.

32.Why did the man say, "perhaps... not that close to them"?
(A) Because those monkeys were pushing him
(B) He wanted the others to follow the rule not to get close to the monkeys.
(C) Because he did not want the others to frighten the monkeys
(D) He's trying to persuade the others to stay away from the monkeys.

33. Which of the following is the closest to "agitated"?
(A) excited
(B) disturbed and upset
(C) adorable and sweet
(D) frightened

34.According to the context of the conversation, why did the woman say, "can't we just have some sushi and seafood"?
(A) She heard that sushi and seafood in Arashiyama are delicious.
(B) Arashiyama is famous for sushi and seafood.

246

(C) She is not interested in seeing monkeys, and would rather do something else.
(D) Seeing those monkeys eating reminds her it's dinner time.

proposal	Budget
A	20 million dollars
B	2 billion dollars
C	20,000,000 dollars

35.Who might these speakers be?
(A) construction workers
(B) bank investors
(C) construction company employees
(D) students studying architecture

36.What is the special situation regarding proposal A?
(A) It did not pass the evaluation by the Department of Environmental Protection
(B) It is being assessed by the Department of Environmental Protection.
(C) The government does not allow construction in that place in proposal A.
(D) Proposal A will cost too much money.

37.What does the woman mean by saying "we haven't reached a consensus …"?
(A) We still need to reach an agreement.
(B) We still need to do more research.
(C) We have reached a conclusion.
(D) We need to carry out more surveys.

247

強化整合答題能力
無懼任何出題陷阱和「結合數個聽力訊息考點」的出題
迅速拆解各式題型

· 包含❶將聽到的訊息轉換成「**形容詞**」的同義轉換❷要「**理解慣用語**」才能選對的試題❸需要綜合訊息後才理解的新聞類話題❹包含「**較為進階**」的計算❺在所提供的聽力訊息有限的情況下，要搭配「**刪去法**」的答題❻部分要理解某些「**進階字彙**」才能答的試題❼區別近似或重疊性的聽力訊息，且容易誤選的試題，詳細釐清題目到底問什麼 ... 等等。

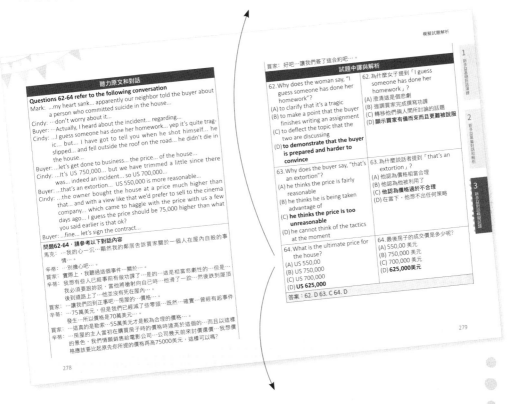

· 掌握上述各類型的出題陷阱和模式，並運用解析強化答題實力，迅速拆解並考取高分。

提高同義詞轉換實力
總是能將聽力訊息對應到關鍵考點
答題力提高 100%

· 聽力訊息稍縱即逝，除了掌握出題規律外，高分的考生都能具備一定程度的同義轉換能力，即能在聽到「一個聽力詞彙或語句」後能迅速對應到「選項的改寫」所以能即刻理解並快速畫卡。

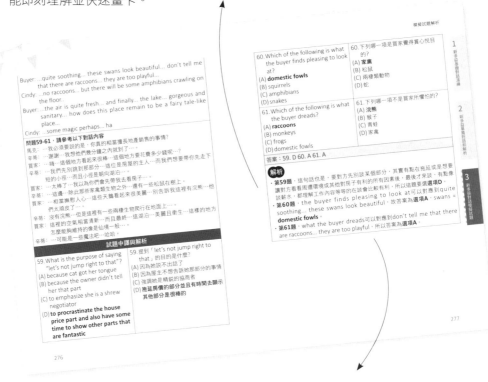

· 書籍中的出題和解析中包含了更多掌握同義轉換的要訣並詳細列於解析中，且以更靈活的出題模式讓考生演練是否都掌握這些考點，應試中更無往不利。

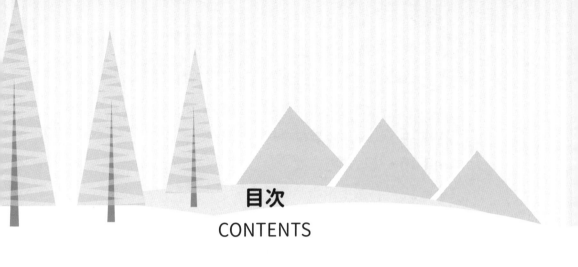

目次
CONTENTS

Part 1 　新多益基礎對話演練

Part 3　新多益對話模擬試題

- 日本嵐山：躁動的猴子讓導遊的話破功
- 建築提案票選：各有優弊，但一切交由董事會決定
- 訂購電影票：四部片，四個電影級別，
  攜帶小朋友就要避開某幾個級別
- 模特兒表現評價：不只是high fashion和commercial之爭
- 整形代言：外貌姣好者有五折折扣只要願意代言即可
- 食安出狀況：樣本受到汙染了
- 非洲之旅：賽倫蓋地相當的悶熱…但願我能有杯椰子水！
- 倍斯特海產貿易公司：哇！餐廳贈送精緻的冰淇淋城堡和蛋糕
- 倍斯特房屋仲介❶：真的是，很會跟買家應對！
- 倍斯特房屋仲介❷：先看看周遭環境、再慢慢進入主題吧！
- 倍斯特房屋仲介❸：買家也做足了功課，要考驗銷售員功力了！
- 倍斯特研究中心：
  法庭判定血液樣本受到汙染，所以這不能用於呈堂的證據
- 倍斯特藥局：藥錠、膠囊、粉末狀藥物還是藥膏呢？

房屋修繕

▶▶ 影子跟讀「短對話」練習 🎧 MP3 001

　　跟著短對話進行跟讀練習和覆誦，強化聽力專注力，現在就一起動身，開始聽「短對話」！

Peter: Hello Mrs. Moore. I came to see you today because I reported the problem of the leaking tap in my bathroom last month, and you promised me the plumber would be here in a few days, but till now he is nowhere to be seen still.

彼得：摩爾太太您好，我今天來是因為我上個月就跟你說過浴室的水龍頭在漏水。你答應我水電工這幾天就會來，可是一直都沒有人來修。

Mrs. Moore: Oh... my apology. I will get onto it on Monday.

摩爾太太：不好意思，我星期一會馬上辦。

Peter: Do you realize how much we have to pay for our last water bill? It cost an extra 50 dollars! I am only a student, and I don't make a lot of money and I hope you are willing to cover the extra cost until the tap is fixed. If the plumber does not rock up on Monday, I will hire one to fix it myself and send the bill to you.

彼得：你知道我們上個月的水費繳多少錢嗎？比平常多50美金。我只是個學生，賺的錢不多，我希望在水龍頭修好之前你要負擔額外的水費。如果水電工星期一再不來修，我只好自己請人來修然後把帳單寄給你。

1 新多益基礎對話演練

2 新多益單篇對話和解析

3 新多益對話模擬試題

房屋修繕

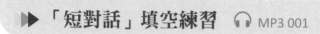

▶▶「短對話」填空練習　🎧 MP3 001

　　利用短對話強化聽力字彙以及拼字能力，答案的話請參照前面的對話喔！

Peter: Hello Mrs. Moore. I came to see you today because I reported the problem of the _____ tap in my __ _____ last month, and you promised me the _____ would be here in a few days, but till now he is nowhere to be seen still.

彼得：摩爾太太您好，我今天來是因為我上個月就跟你説過浴室的水龍頭在漏水。你答應我水電工這幾天就會來，可是一直都沒有人來修。

Mrs. Moore: Oh... my _____ ____. I will get onto it on ____ ____.

摩爾太太：不好意思，我星期一會馬上辦。

Peter: Do you realize how much we have to pay for our last _____? It cost an extra _____! I am only a _____, and I don't make a lot of _____ and I hope you are willing to cover the _____ until the tap is fixed. If the plumber does not rock up on Monday, I will hire one to fix it myself and send _____ to you.

彼得：你知道我們上個月的水費繳多少錢嗎？比平常多50美金。我只是個學生，賺的錢不多，我希望在水龍頭修好之前你要負擔額外的水費。如果水電工星期一再不來修，我只好自己請人來修然後把帳單寄給你。

1 新多益基礎對話演練

2 新多益單篇對話和解析

3 新多益對話模擬試題

UNIT ❷

退租押金

▶▶ 影子跟讀「短對話」練習 🎧 MP3 002

跟著短對話進行跟讀練習和覆誦，強化聽力專注力，現在就一起動身，開始聽「**短對話**」！

Mr. Ferguson: I am happy with the general condition of the wall and the carpet, but the kitchen cabinet doors need to be replaced. The condition is appalling. I will have to deduct USD 150 from your bond.

佛格森先生：這房子的牆面及地毯大概的情況都還好，可是廚房儲物櫃的門需要更換，怎麼會弄得這麼糟？我必須扣你150美金的押金。

Claire: I do apologize, my boyfriend thought the door was jammed and he pulled it too hard. The hinges came off. I think you can easily repair it if you get a handyman

克萊兒：真的很抱歉，我男朋友以為櫥櫃門卡住了就用力拉，誰知道太用力了，櫃子的樞軸就掉下來了。我覺得如果找個雜工來處理應該很容易更換，這應該不需要

in. It would not cost USD 150, would it? I think USD 100 would be a fair price. I mean the condition of the cabinet door was not too flash when we moved in to start with. You can see for yourself we do try to take a good care of this place.

150美金吧！100應該就可以了吧！因為我們搬進來的時候櫥櫃門本來就有點舊，你應該也看的出來我們一直都很照顧這個房子。

退租押金

▶▶ 「短對話」填空練習　🎧 MP3 002

利用短對話強化聽力字彙以及拼字能力，答案的話請參照前面的對話喔！

Mr. Ferguson: I am happy with the general _____ of the _____ and the _____, but the _____ cabinet doors need to be replaced. The condition is appalling. I will have to deduct USD _____ from your _____.

佛格森先生：這房子的牆面及地毯大概的情況都還好，可是廚房儲物櫃的門需要更換，怎麼會弄得這麼糟？我必須扣你150美金的押金。

Claire: I do apologize, my _____ thought _____ was jammed and he pulled it too hard. The _____ came off. I think you can eas-

克萊兒：真的很抱歉，我男朋友以為櫥櫃門卡住了就用力拉，誰知道太用力了，櫃子的樞軸就掉下來了。我覺得如果找個雜工來處理應該

ily repair it if you get a _____ ____ in. It would not cost USD _____, would it? I think USD_____ would be a fair price. I mean the condition of the cabinet door was not too flash when we moved in to start with. You can see for yourself we do try to take a good care of this place.

很容易更換，這應該不需要150美金吧！100應該就可以了吧！因為我們搬進來的時候櫥櫃門本來就有點舊，你應該也看的出來我們一直都很照顧這個房子。

電話安裝紛爭

▶▶ 影子跟讀「短對話」練習 🎧 MP3 003

　　跟著短對話進行跟讀練習和覆誦，強化聽力專注力，現在就一起動身，開始聽「短對話」！

Mark: How is your home phone going?

馬克：你的家用電話都裝好了嗎？

Andy: It is going ok, but I received the bill asking for installation fee, and I remembered clearly there is no installation fee.

安迪：還好，可是我收到一張帳單説要收安裝費，我記得很清楚你説過沒有安裝費的。

Mark: There is no installation fee, if you are switching from other phone company, but for the new client there is an installation charge.

馬克：如果你有安裝過別家公司的電話，那是沒有安裝費的。可是如果是全新用戶那就會有。

Andy: Well, that is not what I was told. I would not have signed up if I knew, there is going to be installation charge. What form do I have to sign to cancel the service?

安迪：可是我聽到的不是這樣，我如果知道有安裝費用我就不會選擇你們公司。那我要取消，要填什麼表格呢？

Mark: I am sorry you are under the wrong impression, let me check with my boss and see what I can do.

馬克：不好意思你可能誤會我的意思，讓我問一下我的上司看能怎麼處理。

Andy: Now you are talking, I am sure you don't want to lose a customer.

安迪：這才對，你一定也不想失去一個客戶。

電話安裝紛爭

▶▶ 「短對話」填空練習 🎧 MP3 003

利用短對話強化聽力字彙以及拼字能力，答案的話請參照前面的對話喔！

Mark: How is your _____ going?

馬克：你的家用電話都裝好了嗎？

Andy: It is going ok, but I received _____ asking for _____, and I remembered clearly there is no _____.

安迪：還好，可是我收到一張帳單說要收安裝費，我記得很清楚你說過沒有安裝費的。

Mark: There is no _____, if you are switching from other phone _____, but for the new client there is an installation charge.

馬克：如果你有安裝過別家公司的電話，那是沒有安裝費的。可是如果是全新用戶那就會有。

Andy: Well, that is not what I was told. I would not have signed up if I knew, there is going to be installation charge. What _____ do I have to sign to cancel the _____?

安迪：可是我聽到的不是這樣，我如果知道有安裝費用我就不會選擇你們公司。那我要取消，要填什麼表格呢？

Mark: I am sorry you are under the wrong _____, let me check with my boss and see what I can do.

馬克：不好意思你可能誤會我的意思，讓我問一下我的上司看能怎麼處理。

Andy: Now you are talking, I am sure you don't want to lose a _____.

安迪：這才對，你一定也不想失去一個客戶。

報價同等品

　　跟著短對話進行跟讀練習和覆誦，強化聽力專注力，現在就一起動身，開始聽「**短對話**」！

Linda: Hey Jamie, I have bad news for you, the part that you enquired yesterday is discontinued, and they do have a replacement, but the maker would need your machine type and serial number to determine whether the new part would suit your machine.

琳達：嗨！傑米，我有個壞的消息要跟你說，你昨天詢價的那個組件已經停產了，原廠是有替代品，可是你需要提供機台號碼還有型號製造商才能確認替代品能不能用在你的機台上。

Jamie: Right, thanks for letting me know, but I don't have the information handy. I need to check with the end

傑米：好的，謝謝你跟我說，我手邊目前沒有這些資訊，我需要跟客戶確認。可能要下星期一或甚至到星期

user and ask them to provide the information. I might have to get back to you on Monday or even Tuesday.

二才能回覆給你。

Linda: No pressure! Just call me back whenever you got the detail.

琳達：沒問題，有資料再打給我就好。

報價同等品

▶ 「短對話」填空練習 🎧 MP3 004

　　利用短對話強化聽力字彙以及拼字能力，答案的話請參照前面的對話喔！

Linda: Hey Jamie, I have bad news for you, the part that you enquired _____ is discontinued, and they do have a _____, but the maker would need your _____ type and _____ to determine whether the _____ would suit your machine.

琳達：嗨！傑米，我有個壞的消息要跟你說，你昨天詢價的那個組件已經停產了，原廠是有替代品，可是你需要提供機台號碼還有型號製造商才能確認替代品能不能用在你的機台上。

Jamie: Right, thanks for letting me know, but I don't have the _____. I need to check with the _____ and

傑米：好的，謝謝你跟我說，我手邊目前沒有這些資訊，我需要跟客戶確認。可能要下星期一或甚至到星期

ask them to provide the information. I might have to get back to you on _____ or even _____.

二才能回覆給你。

Linda: No _____! Just call me back whenever you got the _____.

琳達：沒問題，有資料再打給我就好。

1
新多益基礎對話演練

2
新多益單篇對話和解析

3
新多益對話模擬試題

規格不清楚

▶▶ 影子跟讀「短對話」練習　🎧 MP3 005

　　跟著短對話進行跟讀練習和覆誦，強化聽力專注力，現在就一起動身，開始聽「短對話」！

Tom: Hi Rosie, thanks for the enquiry, but it seems a bit confusing. Can I just go through the details with you please?

湯姆：蘿西您好，謝謝你的詢價單，可是明細有點不清楚，我想跟你再確認一下好嗎？

Rosie: Of course, what seems to be the problem?

蘿西：沒問題，是哪裡不清楚呢？

Tom: The part number that you provided doesn't seem like our standard part number and I double checked the database, it is not our part.

湯姆：你提供的型號不太像我們公司的標準型號，我也重新確認過公司的系統，我們沒有這個型號。

Rosie: Right, can you tell me what your standard part number looks like?

Tom: Sure, for pumps, it normally started with PS34. The number you provided is KS8A, I think it could have been PS34, but you'd better check again with the end user just to be on the safe side.

蘿西：這樣啊，那你可以跟我說你們公司的型號大概是怎麼樣？

湯姆：可以，如果是幫浦的話，通常是PS34開頭的，你給我的型號是KS8A，我猜有可能是PS34，可是你最好跟客戶再確認一下。

1 新多益基礎對話演練

2 新多益單篇對話和解析

3 新多益對話模擬試題

規格不清楚

▶▶「短對話」填空練習 🎧 MP3 005

利用短對話強化聽力字彙以及拼字能力，答案的話請參照前面的對話喔！

Tom: Hi Rosie, thanks for the _____, but it seems a bit _____. Can I just go through the details with you please?

湯姆：蘿西您好，謝謝你的詢價單，可是明細有點不清楚，我想跟你再確認一下好嗎？

Rosie: Of course, what seems to be the _____?

蘿西：沒問題，是哪裡不清楚呢？

Tom: The part number that you provided doesn't seem like our _____ part number and I double checked the _____, it is not our part.

湯姆：你提供的型號不太像我們公司的標準型號，我也重新確認過公司的系統，我們沒有這個型號。

Rosie: Right, can you tell me what your standard part number looks like?

Tom: Sure, for _____, it normally started with _____. The number you provided is _____, I think it could have been _____, but you'd better check again with the end user just to be on the safe side.

蘿西：這樣啊，那你可以跟我說你們公司的型號大概是怎麼樣？

湯姆：可以，如果是幫浦的話，通常是PS34開頭的，你給我的型號是KS8A，我猜有可能是PS34，可是你最好跟客戶再確認一下。

修改規格請重報

跟著短對話進行跟讀練習和覆誦，強化聽力專注力，現在就一起動身，開始聽**「短對話」**！

Gina: Hello, Kevin. How's going? You know the enquiry I sent you the other day for two knife rollers?

吉娜：凱文您好，你記得我前幾天傳給你的詢價單嗎？就是詢價兩個滾刀那張。

Kevin: Yes, I can recall.

凱文：有，我記得。

Gina: I just got off the phone with the client, and they are thinking about replacing the complete cutting unit and upgrading it to the new automatic system. Is it possible for you to send us another

吉娜：客戶剛打來說他們想乾脆把整組的裁切設備更新，升級成最新型的自動系統。你可以幫我報價一組新的裁切設備加上一個備品滾刀？那兩組滾刀就不用報了。

quotation for a completed cutting unit with one spare roller please? Don't worry about those two rollers.

Kevin: Ok, but I have to check whether the new cutting unit can be installed onto your client's machine first. I know some of them are not compatible with the original machine.

凱文： 我知道了，可是我要先查一下新的裁切設備是不是可以裝在你們客戶的機台上，因為有些舊的機型沒有辦法修改。

修改規格請重報

▶▶ 「短對話」填空練習　🎧 MP3 006

　　利用短對話強化聽力字彙以及拼字能力，答案的話請參照前面的對話喔！

Gina: Hello, Kevin. How's going? You know the _____ I sent you the other day for _____?

吉娜：凱文您好，你記得我前幾天傳給你的詢價單嗎？就是詢價兩個滾刀那張。

Kevin: Yes, I can recall.

凱文：有，我記得。

Gina: I just got off the _____ with the _____, and they are thinking about replacing the complete cutting unit and upgrading it to the new _____. Is it possible for you to send us another __

吉娜：客戶剛打來説他們想乾脆把整組的裁切設備更新，升級成最新型的自動系統。你可以幫我報價一組新的裁切設備加上一個備品滾刀？那兩組滾刀就不用報了。

_____ for a completed cutting unit with one _____ please? Don't worry about these two rollers.

Kevin: Ok, but I have to check whether the new cutting unit can be _____ onto your client's _____ first. I know some of them are not _____ with the _____.

凱文：我知道了，可是我要先查一下新的裁切設備是不是可以裝在你們客戶的機台上，因為有些舊的機型沒有辦法修改。

1 新多益基礎對話演練

2 新多益單篇對話和解析

3 新多益對話模擬試題

交期太長
向廠商詢問原因

▶▶ 影子跟讀「短對話」練習 🎧 MP3 007

　　跟著短對話進行跟讀練習和覆誦，強化聽力專注力，現在就一起動身，開始聽**「短對話」**！

Michael: Hi Zoe, thanks for your quotation. I did notice something unusual, and I thought I'd better check with you again.

麥可：柔伊你好，謝謝你的報價，報價單有點不尋常，我想我最好再跟你確認一次。

Zoe: Of course. You are referring to the quotation I sent yesterday if I am not wrong?

柔伊：當然，如果我沒想錯的話，你是指我昨天傳的那張嗎？

Michael: Yeah, that's it.

麥可：是的，沒錯。

Zoe: Oh... what is wrong with

柔伊：噢，是哪裡有問題

it?

呢？

Michael: You know we ordered the same thing last year, but the delivery was only 4 weeks. Is there any reason why the delivery has been pushed back to 8 weeks?

麥可：你知道我們去年有買過同樣的產品，可是那時候交期只有四個星期，為什麼現在變成八星期呢？

Zoe: Right, the thing is, there is a bit of delay in the raw material. We are also waiting for it to arrive before we can start to manufacture.

柔伊：嗯，事情是因為目前原材料的交期有點延誤，我們也還在等東西來才可以開始加工。

交期太長
向廠商詢問原因

▶▶「短對話」填空練習 🎧 MP3 007

利用短對話強化聽力字彙以及拼字能力，答案的話請參照前面的對話喔！

Michael: Hi Zoe, thanks for your _____. I did notice something unusual, and I thought I'd better check with you again.

麥可：柔伊你好，謝謝你的報價，報價單有點不尋常，我想我最好再跟你確認一次。

Zoe: Of course. You are referring to the quotation I sent _____ if I am not wrong?

柔伊：當然，如果我沒想錯的話，你是指我昨天傳的那張嗎？

Michael: Yeah, that's it.

麥可：是的，沒錯。

Zoe: Oh... what is wrong with

柔伊：噢，是哪裡有問題

it?

呢？

Michael: You know we ordered the same thing _____ ____, but the _____ was only _____. Is there any _____ why the delivery has been pushed back to __ _____?

麥可：你知道我們去年有買過同樣的產品，可是那時候交期只有四個星期，為什麼現在變成八星期呢？

Zoe: Right, the thing is, there is a bit of delay in the _____ ____. We are also waiting for it to arrive before we can start to _____.

柔伊：嗯，事情是因為目前原材料的交期有點延誤，我們也還在等東西來才可以開始加工。

替代品再次確認

▶▶ 影子跟讀「短對話」練習　🎧 MP3 008

　　跟著短對話進行跟讀練習和覆誦，強化聽力專注力，現在就一起動身，開始聽「短對話」！

Sandra: Hello Thomas. Thank you for your quotation. I noticed the part number is not what we enquired for, and it was not specified on the quotation. Is this a replacement?

珊卓：湯瑪士您好，謝謝你的報價單，可是我發現你報的型號跟我們詢價的不一樣，而且報價單上沒有特別註明，這是替代品嗎？

Thomas: It is actually an equivalent from a different maker, but the specification is the same as the part that you enquired for. It is 30% cheaper than the original Honeywell one.

湯瑪士：那其實是不同製造商生產的同等品，規格跟你詢價的商品是一樣的，可是價格比原廠漢威公司的便宜了三成。

Sandra: Well, luckily double checked with you before I send the quotation to the client. Can you send me another quotation for the original part, please? I will mention to the end user about the price difference to see if they are willing to switch to the equivalent.

珊卓：嗯，還好我在報價給客戶之前有跟你再次查證，你可以報價一個原廠的產品給我嗎？我會跟使用客戶提一下價格的區別，看看他們是不是願意用同等品。

1 新多益基礎對話演練

2 新多益單篇對話和解析

3 新多益對話模擬試題

替代品再次確認

　　利用短對話強化聽力字彙以及拼字能力，答案的話請參照前面的對話喔！

Sandra: Hello Thomas. Thank you for your quotation. I noticed the _____ is not what we enquired for, and it was not _____ on the quotation. Is this a _____?

珊卓：湯瑪士您好，謝謝你的報價單，可是我發現你報的型號跟我們詢價的不一樣，而且報價單上沒有特別註明，這是替代品嗎？

Thomas: It is actually an _____ from a different maker, but the _____ is the same as the part that you enquired for. It is _____ than the original Honeywell one.

湯瑪士：那其實是不同製造商生產的同等品，規格跟你詢價的商品是一樣的，可是價格比原廠漢威公司的便宜了三成。

Sandra: Well, luckily double checked with you before I send the quotation to the _____. Can you send me another quotation for the original part, please? I will mention to the _____ about the _____ to see if they are willing to _____ to the equivalent.

珊卓：嗯，還好我在報價給客戶之前有跟你再次查證，你可以報價一個原廠的產品給我嗎？我會跟使用客戶提一下價格的區別，看看他們是不是願意用同等品。

下單後要追加數量

　　跟著短對話進行跟讀練習和覆誦，強化聽力專注力，現在就一起動身，開始聽**「短對話」**！

Claire: Hey John, you know that purchase order I sent two days ago for 500 packets of glue. Is it too late to change that to 1000 packets?

克萊兒：你好約翰，你知道我兩天前傳過去的那張500包黏著劑的那張訂單，我可以改成訂1000包嗎？

John: Right, I was just working on the order confirmation for you. You can change it to 1000 packets if you want.

約翰：喔！這樣啊！我剛剛才在處理你的訂單確認書，要改成1000包的話，沒有問題啊。

Claire: Thanks, but I just want to double check whether the

克萊兒：好的，謝謝，可是我想再跟你確認一次這樣的

delivery remains the same as 2 weeks. We would like to consolidate into one shipment to save the shipping cost.

話交期還是維持兩個星期嗎？我們想要跟之前的500包併貨一起出，這樣可以省一筆運費。

John: Let me check our inventory list. Well, I can ship all 1000 packets for you in 3 weeks, would it be ok?

約翰：讓我看一下我們的庫存表，這樣的話我們最快要三個星期的時間才能幫你出貨總計1000包的量，這樣可以接受嗎？

Claire: That would be great. In that case are we entitled to the quantity discount?

克萊兒：這樣沒問題，如果是這樣的話，那你們是不是會給我數量折扣？

John: Of course you are.

約翰：當然可以。

1 新多益基礎對話演練

2 新多益單篇對話和解析

3 新多益對話模擬試題

下單後要追加數量

　　利用短對話強化聽力字彙以及拼字能力，答案的話請參照前面的對話喔！

Claire: Hey John, you know that purchase order I sent two days ago for _____ packets of _____. Is it too late to change that to _____ packets?

克萊兒：你好約翰，你知道我兩天前傳過去的那張500包黏著劑的那張訂單，我可以改成訂1000包嗎？

John: Right, I was just working on the _____ for you. You can change it to 1000 packets if you want.

約翰：喔！這樣啊！我剛剛才在處理你的訂單確認書，要改成1000包的話，沒有問題啊。

Claire: Thanks, but I just want to double check whether the

克萊兒：好的，謝謝，可是我想再跟你確認一次這樣的

_____ remains the same as _____. We would like to consolidate into one ____ _____ to save the _____.

話交期還是維持兩個星期嗎？我們想要跟之前的500包併貨一起出，這樣可以省一筆運費。

John: Let me check our ____ _____. Well, I can ship all 1000 packets for you in ____ _____, would it be ok?

約翰：讓我看一下我們的庫存表，這樣的話我們最快要三個星期的時間才能幫你出貨總計1000包的量，這樣可以接受嗎？

Claire: That would be great. In that case are we entitled to the _____?

克萊兒：這樣沒問題，如果是這樣的話，那你們是不是會給我數量折扣？

John: Of course, you are.

約翰：當然可以。

下單後發現錯誤

跟著短對話進行跟讀練習和覆誦，強化聽力專注力，現在就一起動身，開始聽「**短對話**」！

Jenny: Hello Jimmy, I have an emergency I hope you can help me. Can you put the purchase order that I sent last week on hold for the time being? I just realized the voltage might not be correct, and I have to check with the end user again.

珍妮：阿蘭娜你好，我有件急事需要你的幫忙，你可不可以把我上星期傳過去的訂單先暫停處理？我剛剛發現電壓好像不對，可是我必須再跟客戶確認一次。

Jimmy: Right, I would have to contact the manufacturer and see whether that is possible. I can't guarantee anything at this stage, but I will

吉米：這樣啊，我可能要先問一下製造商看是不是可以先暫停，可是我不能保證一定可以。你什麼時候可以跟我確定電壓的規格？

try my best. When do you think you can get back to me about the correct voltage?

Jenny: I will do it first thing tomorrow for sure. Thanks for trying. I hope I am not in too much trouble.

珍妮：我明天早上會優先處理，謝謝你的好意，希望我沒有闖大禍。

下單後發現錯誤

▶▶ 「短對話」填空練習 🎧 MP3 010

　　利用短對話強化聽力字彙以及拼字能力，答案的話請參照前面的對話喔！

Jenny: Hello Jimmy, I have an _____ I hope you can help me. Can you put the _____ that I sent last week on hold for the time being? I just realized the _____ might not be correct, and I have to check with the _____ again.

珍妮：阿蘭娜你好，我有件急事需要你的幫忙，你可不可以把我上星期傳過去的訂單先暫停處理？我剛剛發現電壓好像不對，可是我必須再跟客戶確認一次。

Jimmy: Right, I would have to contact the _____ and see whether that is possible. I can't _____ anything at this stage, but I will try my

吉米：這樣啊，我可能要先問一下製造商看是不是可以先暫停，可是我不能保證一定可以。你什麼時候可以跟我確定電壓的規格？

best. When do you think you can get back to me about the _____ voltage?

Jenny: I will do it first thing _____ for sure. Thanks for trying. I hope I am not in too much trouble.

珍妮：我明天早上會優先處理，謝謝你的好意，希望我沒有闖大禍。

1 新多益基礎對話演練

2 新多益單篇對話和解析

3 新多益對話模擬試題

提醒合約回傳

跟著短對話進行跟讀練習和覆誦，強化聽力專注力，現在就一起動身，開始聽「**短對話**」！

Jeremy: Hello, this is Jeremy calling from Tai-Guang trading company in Taiwan. I was wondering whether you have received our purchase order number PO100165 dated 13th March 2017.

傑瑞米：您好，我是台灣台光貿易公司的崔西，我想請問一下您有沒有收到我們2017年3月13號傳的訂單呢？訂單號碼是PO100165。

Belinda: Let me check my files. Was it on 13th March?

柏琳達：讓我看一下我的檔案，你是說3月13號傳的嗎？

Jeremy: Yes, it was, and we are still waiting for your order confirmation.

傑瑞米：是的，沒錯。我們一直還在等妳的訂單確認書。

Belinda: Right, is that what you are calling about? Sorry for the delay. I will be on to it, and you should have it by this afternoon.

Jeremy: Thanks for that. Can you also attach a copy of your bank detail please? We haven't had it on record.

Belinda: Sure thing.

柏琳達：好的，請問你特別打電話過來是這個原因嗎？很抱歉耽誤到你的時間，我會馬上處理，你應該今天下午就會收到。

傑瑞米：很謝謝你，可以麻煩你順便傳一份你的匯款帳號給我嗎？我們目前還沒有資料可以留底。

柏琳達：沒問題。

提醒合約回傳

▶▶ 「短對話」填空練習 🎧 MP3 011

利用短對話強化聽力字彙以及拼字能力，答案的話請參照前面的對話喔！

Jeremy: Hello, this is Jeremy calling from Tai-Guang trading company in _____. I was wondering whether you have received our purchase _____ number _____ dated _____.

傑瑞米：您好，我是台灣台光貿易公司的崔西，我想請問一下您有沒有收到我們2017年3月13號傳的訂單呢？訂單號碼是PO100165。

Belinda: Let me check my _____. Was it on 13th March?

柏琳達：讓我看一下我的檔案，你是說3月13號傳的嗎？

Jeremy: Yes, it was, and we are still waiting for your or-

傑瑞米：是的，沒錯。我們一直還在等妳的訂單確認

der _____ .

Belinda: Right, is that what you are calling about? Sorry for the _____ . I will be on to it, and you should have it by this _____ .

Jeremy: Thanks for that. Can you also attach a _____ of your _____ detail please? We haven't had it on record.

Belinda: Sure thing.

書。

柏琳達：好的，請問你特別打電話過來是這個原因嗎？很抱歉耽誤到你的時間，我會馬上處理，你應該今天下午就會收到。

傑瑞米：很謝謝你，可以麻煩你順便傳一份你的匯款帳號給我嗎？我們目前還沒有資料可以留底。

柏琳達：沒問題。

提醒付款條件❶

　　跟著短對話進行跟讀練習和覆誦，強化聽力專注力，現在就一起動身，開始聽「**短對話**」！

Jason: Hello, this is Jason calling from CK trading company in Taiwan. I am ringing regarding an order we received at the beginning of this month from Sue. I was wondering whether I can have a word with her, please?

傑森：您好，我是台灣CK貿易公司的傑森，我有些關於貴公司這個月初訂單的問題要找一下蘇。

Nina: Unfortunately, she is in a meeting at the moment. Can I take a message?

妮娜：不好意思她目前正在開會，您要留話嗎？

Jason: Sure, I would like to check with her whether she put in a request for the down payment to be processed yet. Your order number is 0900234 dated 12th Jan 2017, and the down payment amount is USD 300. Please note the order will only be processed upon receipt of payment.

傑森：好的麻煩你，我想跟她確認一下她有沒有跟會計交代要匯錢的事。貴公司的訂單號碼是0900234，日期是2017年的1月12日。訂金的金額是美金三百塊。麻煩請提醒他訂單要收到訂金之後才會開始處理。

提醒付款條件**1**

利用短對話強化聽力字彙以及拼字能力，答案的話請參照前面的對話喔！

Jason: Hello, this is Jason calling from CK trading company in Taiwan. I am ringing regarding an order we _____ _____ at the beginning of this _____ from Sue. I was wondering whether I can have _____ with her, please?

傑森：您好，我是台灣CK貿易公司的傑森，我有些關於貴公司這個月初訂單的問題要找一下蘇。

Nina: Unfortunately, she is in a _____ at the moment. Can I take a _____?

妮娜：不好意思她目前正在開會，您要留話嗎？

Jason: Sure, I would like to check with her whether she put in a _____ for the _____ to be processed yet. Your order number is _____ dated _____, and the down payment amount is USD _____. Please note the order will only be processed upon _____ of payment.

傑森：好的麻煩你，我想跟她確認一下她有沒有跟會計交代要匯錢的事。貴公司的訂單號碼是0900234，日期是2017年的1月12日。訂金的金額是美金三百塊。麻煩請提醒他訂單要收到訂金之後才會開始處理。

提醒付款條件❷

　　跟著短對話進行跟讀練習和覆誦，強化聽力專注力，現在就一起動身，開始聽「短對話」！

Chris: Hello Miranda, if it's not too much to ask, I am hoping that you can do us a favor.

克里斯：你好，瑪琳達，我希望這不會太麻煩你，我有事要拜託你。

Miranda: Okay. What is it?

瑪琳達：好，你説説看。

Chris: Well, the business is a bit slow in the past few months. We are having a bit of cash flow issues. I was just wondering whether we could come out with new payment terms.

克里斯：是因為這幾個月生意比較不好，我們的現金有點周轉不靈，我是想問妳我們可不可以研商一下是不是可以改一下付款條件。

Miranda: Hmmm, I would have to ask my boss. You know it is purely his call. Just curious, what kind of payment terms are you proposing?

瑪琳達：這個嘛，我要跟我老闆商量一下，你知道這種事都是他決定。只是問一下，你是想要怎麼改？

Chris: If you can put in a good word for us and extend the payment cycle from 60 days to 90 days, then it would be really helpful.

克里斯：如果你可以幫我們跟老闆求個情，讓他同意把60天延長為90天那就太好了。

1 新多益基礎對話演練

2 新多益單篇對話和解析

3 新多益對話模擬試題

提醒付款條件②

　　利用短對話強化聽力字彙以及拼字能力，答案的話請參照前面的對話喔！

Chris: Hello Miranda, if it's not too much to ask, I am hoping that you can do us a ＿＿＿＿＿.

克里斯：你好，瑪琳達，我希望這不會太麻煩你，我有事要拜託你。

Miranda: Okay. What is it?

瑪琳達：好，你説説看。

Chris: Well, the ＿＿＿＿＿ is a bit slow in the past few months. We are having a bit of ＿＿＿＿＿ issues. I was just wondering whether we could come out with ＿＿＿＿＿ terms.

克里斯：是因為這幾個月生意比較不好，我們的現金有點周轉不靈，我是想問妳我們可不可以研商一下是不是可以改一下付款條件。

Miranda: Hmmm, I would have to ask _____. You know it is purely his call. Just curious, what kind of _____ are you proposing?

Chris: If you can put in a good word for us and extend the _____ from _____ days to _____ days, then it would be really helpful.

瑪琳達：這個嘛，我要跟我老闆商量一下，你知道這種事都是他決定。只是問一下，你是想要怎麼改？

克里斯：如果你可以幫我們跟老闆求個情，讓他同意把60天延長為90天那就太好了。

1 新多益基礎對話演練

2 新多益單篇對話和解析

3 新多益對話模擬試題

UNIT ⓮

即將出貨，
請客戶付清尾款

▶▶ 影子跟讀「短對話」練習 🎧 MP3 014

　　跟著短對話進行跟讀練習和覆誦，強化聽力專注力，現在就一起動身，開始聽「**短對話**」！

Sarah: How are you, Justin?

莎拉：你好嗎？賈斯汀？

Justin: I am good, thanks! What can I do for you?

賈斯汀：我很好，謝謝你，可以幫你什麼忙嗎？

Sarah: Just a courtesy call to let you know the shipment is ready for your order number PP88938. The initial payment of USD 500 was received December last year and the remaining balance is USD 1500. Would you be able to arrange the payment for us in

莎拉：我打來是好意提醒你，你訂單PP88938的貨已經好了，我們去年十二月已經收了500美金的訂金，尾款還剩1500美金，可以麻煩你這幾天內幫我們安排付款嗎？

the next few days if possible?

Justin: Sure, not a problem, just do me a favor, can you send us a shipping notice for record keeping purposes, and I will forward it to the accounts for you.

賈斯丁：當然，沒有問題。可以請你幫我個忙嗎，麻煩你傳一張簡短的出貨通知給我做紀錄嗎？我會交代給會計部門。

1 新多益基礎對話演練

2 新多益單篇對話和解析

3 新多益對話模擬試題

即將出貨，
請客戶付清尾款

▶▶ 「短對話」填空練習　🎧 MP3 014

利用短對話強化聽力字彙以及拼字能力，答案的話請參照前面的對話喔！

Sarah: How are you, Olivia?	莎拉：你好嗎？奧莉維亞？
Justin: I am good, thanks! What can I do for you?	賈斯汀：我很好，謝謝你，可以幫你什麼忙嗎？
Sarah: Just a _____ call to let you know the _____ is ready for your order number _____. The initial payment of USD _____ was received _____ last year and the _____ is USD _____. Would you be able to _____ the pay-	莎拉：我打來是好意提醒你，你訂單PP88938的貨已經好了，我們去年十二月已經收了500美金的訂金，尾款還剩1500美金，可以麻煩你這幾天內幫我們安排付款嗎？

ment for us in the next few days if possible?

Justin: Sure, not a problem, just do me a favor, can you send us a shipping _____ for _____ keeping purposes, and I will forward it to the _____ for you.

賈斯丁：當然，沒有問題。可以請你幫我個忙嗎，麻煩你傳一張簡短的出貨通知給我做紀錄嗎？我會交代給會計部門。

UNIT ⑮

匯款單╱會計部門

▶▶影子跟讀「短對話」練習 🎧 MP3 015

　　跟著短對話進行跟讀練習和覆誦，強化聽力專注力，現在就一起動身，開始聽「**短對話**」！

Justin: Hello Sarah, I am calling to let you know the payment has been made on Monday, and you should have it by now.

賈斯丁：你好莎拉，我是打來通知你，尾款已經在星期一匯過去了，你應該已經收到了吧？

Sarah: Oh, thanks for that. would you be able to send me the remittance advice, so we can track the payment with our bank, please?

莎拉：喔！謝謝你幫我處理，你可以把匯款水單傳給我嗎？這樣我可以跟銀行追蹤款項。

Justin: Not a problem. Just to let you know we did instruct

賈斯丁：沒問題，順便跟你說我有交代銀行手續費的部

the bank to cover the bank charge as well. You should receive the exact amount of USD1500.

份我們會負責，你會收到整數1500美金。

Sarah: That's great！The Accounting Department will be pleased. The shipment is ready to go. I will contact the courier, and the shipment will be on its way to you this afternoon.

莎拉：太好了，我們會計會感到滿意。貨已經好了，我會叫快遞來收貨，下午就會出貨給你。

1 新多益基礎對話演練

2 新多益單篇對話和解析

3 新多益對話模擬試題

匯款單／會計部門

▶▶ 「短對話」填空練習 🎧 MP3 015

利用短對話強化聽力字彙以及拼字能力，答案的話請參照前面的對話喔！

Justin: Hello Sarah, I am calling to let you know the ＿＿ ＿＿＿ has been made on ＿ ＿＿＿＿＿, and you should have it by now.

賈斯丁：你好莎拉，我是打來通知你，尾款已經在星期一匯過去了，你應該已經收到了吧？

Sarah: Oh, thanks for that. would you be able to send me the ＿＿＿＿ advice, so we can track the payment with our bank, please?

莎拉：喔！謝謝你幫我處理，你可以把匯款水單傳給我嗎？這樣我可以跟銀行追蹤款項。

Justin: Not a problem. Just to let you know we did instruct

賈斯丁：沒問題，順便跟你說我有交代銀行手續費的部

the _____ cover the _____ as well. You should receive the _____ of USD__ _____.

份我們會負責，你會收到整數1500美金。

Sarah: That's great！The _____ will be pleased. The _____ is ready to go. I will contact the _____, and the shipment will be on its way to you this _____.

莎拉：太好了，我們會計會感到滿意。貨已經好了，我會叫快遞來收貨，下午就會出貨給你。

更改運送方式

▶▶ 影子跟讀「短對話」練習 🎧 MP3 016

跟著短對話進行跟讀練習和覆誦，強化聽力專注力，現在就一起動身，開始聽「**短對話**」！

Pheony: Hi Johnny, I need to make an amendment regarding the shipping method for our PO number 9900384. I'll just quickly run through it with you before I send the new shipping details to you.

費昂妮：強尼您好，我需要更改訂單號碼9900384的運送方式，我先口頭跟你解釋一下再把新運送方式的資料傳給你。

Johnny: Sure, go ahead.

強尼：好的，請說。

Pheony: We were going to use your contracted forwarder, but we decided to go with our courier instead since it

費昂妮：我們本來是要用你們簽約的運送公司，可是我們現在決定要用我們自己的快遞公司去收貨，算起來費

works out about the same but much faster.

用差不多但是比較快。

Johnny: Sure, we can do that, but you know you are still liable for the handling charge.

強尼：當然，我們可以處理，可是要提醒你，這樣的話你還是要付訂單處理費。

Pheony: Yes, I do.

費昂妮：嗯，我知道。

Johnny: Ok then, I will revise the order confirmation once I got the courier details from you.

強尼：好，那等你傳資料過來之後，我在幫你改訂單確認書。

更改運送方式

▶▶ 「短對話」填空練習 🎧 MP3 016

　　利用短對話強化聽力字彙以及拼字能力，答案的話請參照前面的對話喔！

Pheony: Hi Johnny, I need to make an _____ regarding the shipping method for our PO number _____. I'll just quickly run through it with you before I send the new _____ to you.

費昂妮：強尼您好，我需要更改訂單號碼**9900384**的運送方式，我先口頭跟你解釋一下再把新運送方式的資料傳給你。

Johnny: Sure, go ahead.

強尼：好的，請說。

Pheony: We were going to use your _____, but we decided to go with our _____ instead since it works

費昂妮：我們本來是要用你們簽約的運送公司，可是我們現在決定要用我們自己的快遞公司去收貨，算起來費

out about the same but much faster.

用差不多但是比較快。

Johnny: Sure, we can do that, but you know you are still liable for the _____.

強尼：當然，我們可以處理，可是要提醒你，這樣的話你還是要付訂單處理費。

Pheony: Yes, I do.

費昂妮：嗯，我知道。

Johnny: Ok then, I will revise the order confirmation once I got the courier details from you.

強尼：好，那等你傳資料過來之後，我在幫你改訂單確認書。

有急用
請廠商分批出貨

▶▶ 影子跟讀「短對話」練習　🎧 MP3 017

　　跟著短對話進行跟讀練習和覆誦，強化聽力專注力，現在就一起動身，開始聽「**短對話**」！

Mei-Ling: Hello Harrison. I was wondering whether you could help me out. I need to check the progress of one of our orders.

美玲：哈里森您好，你能不能夠幫我一個忙，我想詢問一下我們其中一個訂單的進度。

Harrison: Of course, which order are you referring to?

哈里森：沒問題，你說的是哪一個訂單？

Mei-Ling: The PO number is KK12330. It was for 10 cylinders.

美玲：我們的訂單號碼是KK12330，是十個汽缸。

Harrison: Let me see... Well the order won't be ready for another 3 weeks.

Mei-Ling: I know, but we have a situation here. One of the production lines is down, and the end user desperately needs one to get their machine up and running. Would you be able to check whether you can have any in stock and available for shipping immediately? The rest can wait until then.

哈里森：我看一下，嗯，這個訂單還有三個星期才能供貨。

美玲：我知道，可是我們現在有問題，客戶其中一台的機台壞了，現在使用者急需一個汽缸來替換，你能不能蓋查一下你們有沒有一個現貨可以馬上出貨給我們？其他九個可以等到三個禮拜後再出。

1 新多益基礎對話演練

2 新多益單篇對話和解析

3 新多益對話模擬試題

有急用
請廠商分批出貨

▶▶「短對話」填空練習　🎧 MP3 017

　　利用短對話強化聽力字彙以及拼字能力，答案的話請參照前面的對話喔！

Mei-Ling: Hello Harrison. I was wondering whether you could help me out. I need to check the ＿＿＿＿＿ of one of our orders.

美玲：哈里森您好，你能不能夠幫我一個忙，我想詢問一下我們其中一個訂單的進度。

Harrison: Of course, which order are you referring to?

哈里森：沒問題，你說的是哪一個訂單？

Mei-Ling: The PO number is ＿＿＿＿＿. It was for ＿＿＿＿＿.

美玲：我們的訂單號碼是KK12330，是十個汽缸。

Harrison: Let me see... Well the order won't be ready for another _____ .

哈里森：我看一下，嗯，這個訂單還有三個星期才能供貨。

Mei-Ling: I know, but we have a _____ here. One o f the _____ lines is down, and the end user desperately needs one to get their _____ up and running. Would you be able to check whether you can have any _____ and available for _____ immediately? The rest can wait until then.

美玲：我知道，可是我們現在有問題，客戶其中一台的機台壞了，現在使用者急需一個汽缸來替換，你能不能蓋查一下你們有沒有一個現貨可以馬上出貨給我們？其他九個可以等到三個禮拜後再出。

確認運送方式

▶▶ **影子跟讀「短對話」練習** 🎧 MP3 018

　　跟著短對話進行跟讀練習和覆誦，強化聽力專注力，現在就一起動身，開始聽**「短對話」**！

Fred: Hi Emma, just to let you know your order number 835001 is ready to be picked up. I just noticed that you haven't specified the shipping method on your PO, do you want us to courier it or send it via a forwarder.

佛萊德：艾瑪您好，我是想通知您貴公司的835001號訂單已經可以出貨了，可是我發現你們訂單上並沒有註明要用何種運送方式，您想要用快遞出貨還是要用海運出貨呢？

Emma: Right, my apology. Please hold on a second, let me check. Do you happen to know the dimensions of the package?

艾瑪：喔，這樣啊，很抱歉我疏忽了。請您稍等一下，我來看看。請問貨品的外包裝的尺寸是多少？

Fred: Yes, it is 120×90×50 cm, and the weight is approximately 25 kilos.

佛萊德：嗯，是120×90×50公分，總重大概是 25公斤。

Emma: In that case, please use our CPS to collect account. Our account number is: XX659922.

艾瑪：這樣的話，麻煩您用我們CPS快遞的對方付款帳號來出貨，帳號是：XX659922。

1 新多益基礎對話演練

2 新多益單篇對話和解析

3 新多益對話模擬試題

確認運送方式

▶▶ 「短對話」填空練習 🎧 MP3 018

利用短對話強化聽力字彙以及拼字能力，答案的話請參照前面的對話喔！

Fred: Hi Emma, just to let you know your order number _____ is ready to be picked up. I just noticed that you haven't specified the _____ method on your PO, do you want us to courier it or send it via a _____.

佛萊德：艾瑪您好，我是想通知您貴公司的835001號訂單已經可以出貨了，可是我發現你們訂單上並沒有註明要用何種運送方式，您想要用快遞出貨還是要用海運出貨呢？

Emma: Right, my apology. Please hold on a second, let me check. Do you happen to know the _____ of the _____?

艾瑪：喔，這樣啊，很抱歉我疏忽了。請您稍等一下，我來看看。請問貨品的外包裝的尺寸是多少？

Fred: Yes, it is _____ cm, and the weight is approximately _____ .

Emma: In that case, please use our CPS to collect account. Our _____ number is: _____ .

佛萊德：嗯，是120×90×50公分，總重大概是 25公斤。

艾瑪：這樣的話，麻煩您用我們CPS快遞的對方付款帳號來出貨，帳號是：XX659922。

收到錯誤的商品，要求更換

▶▶ 影子跟讀「短對話」練習　🎧 MP3 019

　　跟著短對話進行跟讀練習和覆誦，強化聽力專注力，現在就一起動身，開始聽「短對話」！

Terry: Hello Lucy, there is a problem here. We received the conveyor belt yesterday, but the design is wrong. The build-in magnet was supposed to be on the right side, but it was on the left.

泰瑞：露西您好，我們現在有個問題，輸送帶昨天收到了，可是設計上有錯。裡面內建的磁鐵應該是要在右邊，不是左邊。

Lucy: Right, let me check the order. Did you point out which side the magnet is meant to be on?

露西：這樣啊，讓我檢查一下你們的訂單，你有在訂單上有特別註明嗎？

Terry: Yes, we did. The con-

泰瑞：當然有，我們三年前

veyor belt is meant to be the replacement for the one we ordered 3 years ago. With the magnet on the wrong side, there is no way we can use this.

訂過一樣的輸送帶，而這個新的輸送帶是要來更換舊的這個。所以如果磁鐵方向做錯，我們就沒辦法用這個東西了。

Lucy: Well, I would have to check with the engineering department and see what we can do. Do you mind shipping the conveyor back?

露西：我知道了，我會跟工程部門討論，看能怎麼處理。你介意把東西退回來嗎？

收到錯誤的商品，要求更換

▶▶ 「短對話」填空練習 🎧 MP3 019

利用短對話強化聽力字彙以及拼字能力，答案的話請參照前面的對話喔！

Terry: Hello Lucy, there is a problem here. We received the ＿＿＿＿＿ yesterday, but the ＿＿＿＿＿ is wrong. The build-in ＿＿＿＿＿ was supposed to be on the ＿＿＿＿＿ side, but it was on the ＿＿＿＿＿.

泰瑞：露西您好，我們現在有個問題，輸送帶昨天收到了，可是設計上有錯。裡面內建的磁鐵應該是要在右邊，不是左邊。

Lucy: Right, let me check the ＿＿＿＿＿. Did you point out which side the magnet is meant to be on?

露西：這樣啊，讓我檢查一下你們的訂單，你有在訂單上有特別註明嗎？

Terry: Yes, we did. The conveyor belt is meant to be the _____ for the one we ordered _____. With the magnet on the wrong side, there is no way we can use this.

Lucy: Well, I would have to check with the _____ department and see what we can do. Do you mind shipping the _____ back?

泰瑞：當然有，我們三年前訂過一樣的輸送帶，而這個新的輸送帶是要來更換舊的這個。所以如果磁鐵方向做錯，我們就沒辦法用這個東西了。

露西：我知道了，我會跟工程部門討論，看能怎麼處理。你介意把東西退回來嗎？

運送過程損壞，向國外反應

▶▶ 影子跟讀「短對話」練習　🎧 MP3 020

　　跟著短對話進行跟讀練習和覆誦，強化聽力專注力，現在就一起動身，開始聽「**短對話**」！

Sam: Hello, Lyndsay, thanks for the shipment, we received it yesterday. But 1 of the temperature gauges is damaged. The protecting glass is broken, can you replace them?

山姆：琳希您好，謝謝你幫我們出貨，我們昨天收到了，可是其中的一個溫度計有破損，上面的保護鏡破掉了，你可以幫我們更換嗎？

Lyndsay: Just one out of ten? Yes, we can replace them, but we are not responsible for the additional shipping cost.

琳希：十個裡面破了一個嗎？沒問題，我們可以更換，可是額外的運費要你們自付。

Sam: Yes, I can understand that.

Lyndsay: Can you arrange for the broken one to be returned, please?

Sam: Definitely. Since I've got you on the phone, can you check whether you have 1 available for shipping immediately?

Lyndsay: Unfortunately, we don't have any at the moment, but the next batch will be ready in two days. I can organize 1 to go out to you straight away if that helps.

Sam: That would be great.

山姆：好，這個我了解。

琳希：可以麻煩你把破的那個寄回來嗎？

山姆：那當然，既然你在線上，我可以順便詢問一下你們是否有一個現貨可以馬上出？

琳希：不好意思沒有，可是下一批貨兩天後就會好，我可以馬上幫你寄個去如果你要的話。

山姆：好的，那麻煩你。

運送過程損壞，向國外反應

▶▶ 「短對話」填空練習 🎧 MP3 020

　　利用短對話強化聽力字彙以及拼字能力，答案的話請參照前面的對話喔！

Sam: Hello, Lyndsay, thanks for the ＿＿＿＿＿, we received it yesterday. But 1 of the ＿＿＿＿＿ gauges is ＿＿＿＿＿. The ＿＿＿＿＿ is broken, can you replace them?

山姆：琳希您好，謝謝你幫我們出貨，我們昨天收到了，可是其中的一個溫度計有破損，上面的保護鏡破掉了，你可以幫我們更換嗎？

Lyndsay: Just one out of ten? Yes, we can replace them, but we are not responsible for the ＿＿＿＿＿.

琳希：十個裡面破了一個嗎？沒問題，我們可以更換，可是額外的運費要你們自付。

Sam: Yes, I can understand that.

山姆：好，這個我了解。

Lyndsay: Can you arrange for the broken one to be returned, please?

琳希：可以麻煩你把破的那個寄回來嗎？

Sam: Definitely. Since I've got you one the _____, can you check whether you have _____ available for _____ immediately?

山姆：那當然，既然你在線上，我可以順便詢問一下你們是否有一個現貨可以馬上出？

Lyndsay: Unfortunately, we don't have any at the moment, but the next _____ will be ready in _____. I can organize 1 to go out to you straight away if that helps.

琳希：不好意思沒有，可是下一批貨兩天後就會好，我可以馬上幫你寄個去如果你要的話。

Sam: That would be great.

山姆：好的，那麻煩你。

UNIT ㉑

海運航班接不上，無法準時交貨

▶▶ 影子跟讀「短對話」練習　🎧 MP3 021

　　跟著短對話進行跟讀練習和覆誦，強化聽力專注力，現在就一起動身，開始聽**「短對話」**！

Linda: Hi Jimmy, I just heard from the forwarder, the shipment was scheduled to arrive in Kaohsiung port on 25th Mar, but there is a delay in Singapore. Looks like the shipping vessel would hang around Singapore for extra 3-4 days.

琳達：吉米你好，我聽我們船運公司說貨輪本來是預計3月25日抵達高雄港，可是在新加坡有些問題耽誤了，看來可能在新加坡會多耽誤3到4天。

Jimmy: Right! Thanks for letting me know. I think extra 3 or 4 days would not cause any problem, but if it is longer than a week, then we

吉米：這樣啊！謝謝你通知我，如果只是三、四天那倒是還好，只要不要超過一個星期，因為我們可能會因延誤交期而有麻煩。

might be in trouble for missing the deadline.

Linda: There is nothing we can do other than wait. I will keep an eye on this case, but I will keep you posted when I know more.

琳達：目前我們只能等，我會特別注意這個案子，有消息我會隨時跟你聯絡。

海運航班接不上，無法準時交貨

▶▶ 「短對話」填空練習 中標　 MP3 021

　　利用短對話強化聽力字彙以及拼字能力，答案的話請參照前面的對話喔！

Linda: Hi Jimmy, I just heard from the _____, the shipment was scheduled to arrive in _____ port on _____, but there is a delay in _____. Looks like the _____ would hang around _____ for extra 3-4 days.

琳達：吉米你好，我聽我們船運公司說貨輪本來是預計3月25日抵達高雄港，可是在新加坡有些問題耽誤了，看來可能在新加坡會多耽誤3到4天。

Jimmy: Right! Thanks for letting me know. I think extra 3 or 4 days would not cause any problem, but if it is longer than _____, then we might be in trouble for missing the _____

吉米：這樣啊！謝謝你通知我，如果只是三、四天那倒是還好，只要不要超過一個星期，因為我們可能會因延誤交期而有麻煩。

____.

Linda: There is nothing we can do other than wait. I will keep an eye on this case, but I will keep you posted when I know more.

琳達：目前我們只能等，我會特別注意這個案子，有消息我會隨時跟你聯絡。

收到的貨物與出貨單內容不符

▶▶ 影子跟讀「短對話」練習　🎧 MP3 022

　　跟著短對話進行跟讀練習和覆誦，強化聽力專注力，現在就一起動身，開始聽「**短對話**」！

Michelle: Thanks for the shipment, but I think there is a problem. This is not the right order for us.

蜜雪兒：謝謝你的出貨，可是這批貨有點問題，這跟我們訂的貨不一樣。

Justin: Right, can you explain further, please?

賈斯丁：是嗎？可以說清楚一點嗎？

Michelle: Sure, do you have a copy of the packing list handy?

蜜雪兒：當然，你手邊有我們的出貨單嗎？

Justin: Just a minute, I will

賈斯丁：稍等，我找一下，

look it up. Here it is.

找到了。

Michelle: On the packing list it shows that we ordered a complete filter system which is housing plus a filter pad, but what we received is only a filter pad replacement. Can you please check your record and send us the filter housing ASAP please?

蜜雪兒： 在出貨單上顯示我們訂的是整組的過濾器，就是過濾器再加上濾網，可是實際上貨物裡面只有濾網。你可以查一下你的出貨紀錄然後趕快補一個過濾器給我們嗎？

Justin: Ok, I will check with my coworker and let you know shortly.

賈斯丁： 好的，我跟我的同事求證一下再跟你說。

UNIT ㉒

收到的貨物與
出貨單內容不符

▶「短對話」填空練習　🎧 MP3 022

　　利用短對話強化聽力字彙以及拼字能力，答案的話請參照前面的對話喔！

Michelle: Thanks for the shipment, but I think there is a _____. This is not the _____ for us.

蜜雪兒：謝謝你的出貨，可是這批貨有點問題，這跟我們訂的貨不一樣。

Justin: Right, can you explain further, please?

賈斯丁：是嗎？可以說清楚一點嗎？

Michelle: Sure, do you have a _____ of the packing list handy?

蜜雪兒：當然，你手邊有我們的出貨單嗎？

Justin: Just a minute, I will

賈斯丁：稍等，我找一下，

look it up. Here it is.

找到了。

Michelle: On the _____ it shows that we ordered a _____ system which is housing plus a filter pad, but what we received is only a filter pad replacement. Can you please check your _____ and send us the filter housing ASAP please?

蜜雪兒： 在出貨單上顯示我們訂的是整組的過濾器，就是過濾器再加上濾網，可是實際上貨物裡面只有濾網。你可以查一下你的出貨紀錄然後趕快補一個過濾器給我們嗎？

Justin: Ok, I will check with my _____ and let you know shortly.

賈斯丁： 好的，我跟我的同事求證一下再跟你説。

供應商來訪

▶▶ 影子跟讀「短對話」練習　🎧 MP3 023

　　跟著短對話進行跟讀練習和覆誦，強化聽力專注力，現在就一起動身，開始聽「短對話」！

Cherry: Hello Jason, I was wondering whether Mr. Tseng would be available at 10:00 on 5th of July. Mr. Robinson would like to have a meeting with him to discuss the Da-Ling project. I will send you the agenda shortly.

佳麗：你好，傑森，請問曾先生七月五日早上十點有空嗎？羅賓森先生想跟他討論一下大林專案，我晚一點把會議要討論的事項傳給你。

Jason: Let me check his schedule. He has a meeting booked with our sales manager this morning, is Mr. Robinson free that after-

傑森：讓我看一下他的行程，嗯，他早上要跟我們的業務經理開會，羅賓森先生下午有空嗎？兩點好不好？

noon? Say 2 pm?

Cherry: He has a lunch meeting with someone else, and they should be done around 2 pm. Can you book him in for 3 pm then?

佳麗：他中午跟其他人有約，大概兩點會好，那約三點好嗎？

Jason: I sure can. Does he have a dinner plan? If not, I am sure Mr.Tseng would like to take him out for dinner.

傑森：當然可以，他晚餐有約人了嗎？不然曾先生想請他吃飯。

供應商來訪

▶▶ 「短對話」填空練習 🎧 MP3 023

利用短對話強化聽力字彙以及拼字能力，答案的話請參照前面的對話喔！

Cherry: Hello Jason, I was wondering whether Mr. Tseng would be available at 10:00 on _____. Mr. Robinson would like to have a __ _____ with him to discuss the Da-Ling project. I will send you the _____ shortly.

佳麗：你好，傑森，請問曾先生七月五日早上十點有空嗎？羅賓森先生想跟他討論一下大林專案，我晚一點把會議要討論的事項傳給你。

Jason: Let me check his _____. He has a meeting booked with our _____ this _____, is Mr. Robinson free that afternoon? Say

傑森：讓我看一下他的行程，嗯，他早上要跟我們的業務經理開會，羅賓森先生下午有空嗎？兩點好不好？

2 pm?

Cherry: He has a lunch meeting with someone else, and they should be done around 2 pm. Can you book him in for _____ then?

Jason: I sure can. Does he have a dinner plan? If not, I am sure Mr.Tseng would like to take him out for _____.

佳麗：他中午跟其他人有約，大概兩點會好，那約三點好嗎？

傑森：當然可以，他晚餐有約人了嗎？不然曾先生想請他吃飯。

1 新多益基礎對話演練

2 新多益單篇對話和解析

3 新多益對話模擬試題

飛機延誤需更改行程及接機

▶▶ 影子跟讀「短對話」練習　🎧 MP3 024

跟著短對話進行跟讀練習和覆誦，強化聽力專注力，現在就一起動身，開始聽「**短對話**」！

Tammy: Hi Frank, I am sorry for calling so late. I am calling to let you know that Mr. Rollings missed the connecting flight for tomorrow morning, and he won't get in until around 11:00 am. Can you push the meeting back by a day and reschedule it to the day after?

潭美：你好法蘭克，很抱歉這麼晚打給你，我是想通知你羅倫斯先生在曼谷機場的班機沒接上，他們重新幫他訂了明天早上的飛機，可是他要早上11點才會到，可以麻煩你把原來的會議推遲一天改成後天嗎？

Frank: Thanks for letting me know. From what I can recall, I think Mr. Wu would be free the day after. It should not

法蘭克：謝謝你通知我，我記得吳先生後天有空，應該沒有問題。可以告訴我他們班機號碼嗎？我會通知司機

be a problem. Can you let me know the flight number please? I will notify the driver, so he will be there to pick him up when he arrives.

在他抵達機場時會去接他。

飛機延誤需更改行程及接機

▶▶ 「短對話」填空練習 🎧 MP3 024

利用短對話強化聽力字彙以及拼字能力，答案的話請參照前面的對話喔！

Tammy: Hi Frank, I am sorry for calling so late. I am calling to let you know that Mr. Rollings missed the _____ for _____ morning, and he won't get in until _____. Can you push the meeting back by a day and _____ it to the day after?

潭美：你好法蘭克，很抱歉這麼晚打給你，我是想通知你羅倫斯先生在曼谷機場的班機沒接上，他們重新幫他訂了明天早上的飛機，可是他要早上11點才會到，可以麻煩你把原來的會議推遲一天改成後天嗎？

Frank: Thanks for letting me know. From what I can recall, I think Mr. Wu would be _____ the day after. It should not be a problem. Can you

法蘭克：謝謝你通知我，我記得吳先生後天有空，應該沒有問題。可以告訴我他們班機號碼嗎？我會通知司機在他抵達機場時會去接他。

let me know the _____
please? I will notify the ____
_____, so he will be there to
pick him up when he arrives.

討論會議中談論的事項執行進度

▶▶ 影子跟讀「短對話」練習 🎧 MP3 025

　　跟著短對話進行跟讀練習和覆誦，強化聽力專注力，現在就一起動身，開始聽**「短對話」**！

Tammy: Hi Jimmy, has Mr. Wu spoken to you regarding the specifications of the Da-Ling project? Apparently, he told me Mr. Rollings will forward it to him.

潭美：蘇西您好，吳先生有沒有跟你說過關於大林專案的詳細計劃書？顯然，羅倫斯先生有跟吳先生提過專案會轉交給他。

Jimmy: Yes, I am working on it at the moment. There are a few amendments that need to be done and Mr. Wu also wants to add a few things in it. I should have it ready by next Tuesday.

吉米：有的！我現在正在處理，不過還有點地方要修改，吳先生還有東西要新增，我應該下禮拜二就可以給你。

Tammy: That would be great. Do you have a copy of the meeting minutes that I can have? Just in case I missed anything.

潭美：那太好了，我可以順便跟你要一份會議紀錄嗎？我可以對照一下，怕我疏忽掉其他的東西。

Jimmy: Definitely, I will send it to you straight away.

吉米：當然可以，這個我馬上就可以傳給你。

1 新多益基礎對話演練

2 新多益單篇對話和解析

3 新多益對話模擬試題

討論會議中談論的事項執行進度

▶▶「短對話」填空練習 🎧 MP3 025

利用短對話強化聽力字彙以及拼字能力，答案的話請參照前面的對話喔！

Tammy: Hi Jimmy, has Mr. Wu spoken to you regarding the _____ of the Da-Ling _____? Apparently, he told me Mr. Rollings will _____ it to him.

潭美：蘇西您好，吳先生有沒有跟你說過關於大林專案的詳細計劃書？顯然，羅倫斯先生有跟吳先生提過專案會轉交給他。

Jimmy: Yes, I am working on it at the moment. There are a few _____ that need to be done and Mr. Wu also wants to add a few things in it. I should have it ready by _____.

吉米：有的！我現在正在處理，不過還有點地方要修改，吳先生還有東西要新增，我應該下禮拜二就可以給你。

Tammy: That would be great. Do you have a _____ of the _____ that I can have? Just in case I missed anything.

潭美：那太好了，我可以順便跟你要一份會議紀錄嗎？我可以對照一下，怕我疏忽掉其他的東西。

Jimmy: Definitely, I will send it to you straight away.

吉米：當然可以，這個我馬上就可以傳給你。

1 新多益基礎對話演練

2 新多益單篇對話和解析

3 新多益對話模擬試題

訪客的喜好／
注意事項

　　跟著短對話進行跟讀練習和覆誦，強化聽力專注力，現在就一起動身，開始聽「短對話」！

Mark: Hey Belinda, I am making a reservation for lunch for Mr. Moss. Does he have any special dietary requirements?

馬克：柏琳達您好，我現在要幫摩斯先生安排午餐的餐廳，請問他有沒有什麼東西不吃的？

Belinda: No, he is pretty easy, but he does prefer a light lunch. As much as he enjoys Taiwanese food, he would prefer a sandwich and salad for lunch.

柏琳達：沒有，他還蠻隨和的，但他中午習慣吃清淡一點。雖然他喜歡台菜，可是午餐他還是偏好吃三明治和沙拉。

Mark: Right, I think in that

馬克：好的，既然這樣的話

case I will book a western restaurant for lunch then. Is there anything else we can pre arrange for him?

那我中餐就訂西餐廳，還有什麼其他的事需要先幫他準備的嗎？

Belinda: Yes, he would prefer to stay in a smoking room actually. Would this be a problem?

柏琳達：有，可以麻煩你幫他訂可以抽菸的房間嗎？這會有問題嗎？

Mark: Well, I will check with the hotel, if not, I can find another hotel for him.

馬克：嗯，我來問一下飯店，如果不行的話我就幫他找另一間飯店。

訪客的喜好／注意事項

▶▶ 「短對話」填空練習　🎧 MP3 026

　　利用短對話強化聽力字彙以及拼字能力，答案的話請參照前面的對話喔！

Mark: Hey Belinda, I am making a _____ for _____ for Mr. Moss. Does he have any _____?

馬克：柏琳達您好，我現在要幫摩斯先生安排午餐的餐廳，請問他有沒有什麼東西不吃的？

Belinda: No, he is pretty easy, but he does prefer a light lunch. As much as he enjoys _____, he would prefer a _____ and _____ for lunch.

柏琳達：沒有，他還蠻隨和的，但他中午習慣吃清淡一點。雖然他喜歡台菜，可是午餐他還是偏好吃三明治和沙拉。

Mark: Right, I think in that case I will book a _____ for lunch then. Is there anything

馬克：好的，既然這樣的話那我中餐就訂西餐廳，還有什麼其他的事需要先幫他準

else we can pre arrange for him?

備的嗎？

Belinda: Yes, he would prefer to stay in a _____ actually. Would this be a problem?

柏琳達：有，可以麻煩你幫他訂可以抽菸的房間嗎？這會有問題嗎？

Mark: Well, I will check with the _____, if not, I can find another _____ for him.

馬克：嗯，我來問一下飯店，如果不行的話我就幫他找另一間飯店。

1 新多益基礎對話演練

2 新多益單篇對話和解析

3 新多益對話模擬試題

與訪客確認行程

▶▶ 影子跟讀「短對話」練習　🎧 MP3 027

　　跟著短對話進行跟讀練習和覆誦，強化聽力專注力，現在就一起動身，開始聽「**短對話**」！

Yvonne: Hi Jimmy, I was wondering if Mr. Harvey's schedule to Taiwan is finalized?

伊凡：吉米您好，我想請問哈維先生的台灣行程都定案了嗎？

Jimmy: More or less, his accommodations are confirmed. He is booked in to stay in Holiday Inn for two nights. The driver will pick him up from the airport the night to the 25th, and take him to the hotel. I am just waiting to hear back from this other client, to see if

吉米：差不多了，飯店訂好了，他會在假日飯店住兩晚。司機在25號晚上會去接他，然後帶他去飯店。我還在等他其他客戶的確認，看看他們是不是27號早上有空，然後我就可以傳一份行程表給你。

they are available in the morning of the 27th, then I will be able to send you the completed schedule.

Yvonne: Sounds good. Thank you so much for your help.

伊凡：太好了！謝謝你的幫忙。

UNIT 27

與訪客確認行程

▶▶ 「短對話」填空練習 🎧 MP3 027

　　利用短對話強化聽力字彙以及拼字能力，答案的話請參照前面的對話喔！

Yvonne: Hi Jimmy, I was wondering if Mr. Harvey's ___ _____ to Taiwan is final-ized?

伊凡：吉米您好，我想請問哈維先生的台灣行程都定案了嗎？

Jimmy: More or less, his _____ _____ are confirmed. He is booked in to stay in _____ __ for _____. The _____ ___ will pick him up from the _____ the night to the 25th, and take him to the __ _____. I am just waiting to hear back from this other __ _____, to see if they are

吉米：差不多了，飯店訂好了，他會在假日飯店住兩晚。司機在25號晚上會去接他，然後帶他去飯店。我還在等他其他客戶的確認，看看他們是不是27號早上有空，然後我就可以傳一份行程表給你。

available in the _____ of the 27th, then I will be able to send you the _____.

Yvonne: Sounds good. Thank you so much for your help.

伊凡：太好了！謝謝你的幫忙。

廠商想直接拜訪客戶

▶▶ 影子跟讀「短對話」練習　🎧 MP3 028

　　跟著短對話進行跟讀練習和覆誦，強化聽力專注力，現在就一起動身，開始聽「**短對話**」！

Kelly: Hi Johnny, I know you are in the process of sorting the schedule. I was wondering if it's possible to set up a meeting with Tung-Seng company. Mr. Pence would like to do a sales presentation on our latest model.

凱莉：強尼您好，我知道你正為我們的來訪做準備，我是想問你，有沒有機會可以跟東盛公司見個面，因為彭斯先生想跟他們介紹我們最新的設備。

Johnny: Well, I would have to check with Mrs. Lee first. She normally does not involve the supplier directly with our clients.

強尼：這個嘛，我要先問一下李女士，因為通常她是不會帶廠商去見客戶的。

Kelly: It will be really helpful If you can check with Mrs. Lee. Mr. Pence believes it will be beneficial.

凱莉：好啊，那就麻煩你幫我們跟她溝通一下，因為彭斯先生覺得對商議上會很有幫助。

Johnny: Sure, I will check with her, but I will be honest with you, but it's very unlikely.

強尼：好的，我會幫你問，可是老實說，但是實在是不太可能。

廠商想直接拜訪客戶

▶▶「短對話」填空練習 🎧 MP3 028

利用短對話強化聽力字彙以及拼字能力，答案的話請參照前面的對話喔！

Kelly: Hi Johnny, I know you are in the _____ of sorting the schedule. I was wondering if it's possible to set up a meeting with Tung-Seng _____. Mr. Pence would like to do a _____ on our latest _____.

凱莉：強尼您好，我知道你正為我們的來訪做準備，我是想問你，有沒有機會可以跟東盛公司見個面，因為彭斯先生想跟他們介紹我們最新的設備。

Johnny: Well, I would have to check with Mrs. Lee first. She normally does not involve the _____ directly with our clients.

強尼：這個嘛，我要先問一下李女士，因為通常她是不會帶廠商去見客戶的。

Kelly: It will be really helpful If you can _____ with Mrs. Lee. Mr. Pence believes it will be _____.

Johnny: Sure, I will check with her, but I will be _____ with you, but it's very unlikely.

凱莉：好啊，那就麻煩你幫我們跟她溝通一下，因為彭斯先生覺得對商議上會很有幫助。

強尼：好的，我會幫你問，可是老實說，但是實在是不太可能。

私人光觀行程

▶▶ 影子跟讀「短對話」練習 🎧 MP3 029

跟著短對話進行跟讀練習和覆誦，強化聽力專注力，現在就一起動身，開始聽**「短對話」**！

Yvonne: Thanks for making all the appointments for Mr. Harvey, and there is one more thing. Do you think you can book a couple of nights of accommodation in Kenting for him as well? He would like to stay on for a bit of holiday.

伊凡：謝謝你幫哈維先生安排行程，還有一件事要麻煩你，你可以幫他在墾丁訂兩個晚上的住宿嗎？他想要順便度個假。

Jimmy: Not a problem, what kind of accommodation is he after?

吉米：沒問題，他想要怎樣的房型？

Yvonne: He would prefer to stay in a resort type of accommodation, price range between 150 EURO −200 EURO per night.

伊凡：他喜歡住度假村類型飯店，預算大概是每個晚上150到200歐元左右。

Jimmy: Sure, there are lots to choose from. I will send you some information and you can let me know which one to book for him.

吉米：好的，那他的選擇還不少，我再傳一些飯店的資料給你，你再跟我説要幫他訂哪一間。

1 新多益基礎對話演練

2 新多益單篇對話和解析

3 新多益對話模擬試題

UNIT ㉙

私人光觀行程

▶▶「短對話」填空練習 🎧 MP3 029

利用短對話強化聽力字彙以及拼字能力，答案的話請參照前面的對話喔！

Yvonne: Thanks for making all the _____ for Mr. Harvey, and there is one more thing. Do you think you can book a couple of nights of _____ for him as well? He would like to stay on for a bit of holiday.

伊凡：謝謝你幫哈維先生安排行程，還有一件事要麻煩你，你可以幫他在墾丁訂兩個晚上的住宿嗎？他想要順便度個假。

Jimmy: Not a problem, what kind of accommodation is he after?

吉米：沒問題，他想要怎樣的房型？

Yvonne: He would prefer to

伊凡：他喜歡住度假村類型

stay in a resort type of ac-commodation, _____ be-tween _____ EURO –____ _____ EURO per night.

飯店，預算大概是每個晚上150到200歐元左右。

Jimmy: Sure, there are lots to choose from. I will send you some _____ and you can let me know which one to book for him.

吉米：好的，那他的選擇還不少，我再傳一些飯店的資料給你，你再跟我説要幫他訂哪一間。

詢問工程師行程表

▶▶ 影子跟讀「短對話」練習 🎧 MP3 030

跟著短對話進行跟讀練習和覆誦，強化聽力專注力，現在就一起動身，開始聽**「短對話」**！

Peggy: So do you know which engineers will be coming to do the installation yet?

佩琪：那你知道是哪幾個工程師會來安裝了嗎？

Dexter: Well, at the moment I got Andrew and Clive available, I know you prefer Mark, but he won't be available until the end of May. I don't think the end user can wait that long.

戴斯特：嗯，目前只有安德路還有克萊夫有空，我知道你比較想要馬克去，可是他要到五月底才會有空。我不認為客戶能夠等這麼久。

Peggy: Yes, they are in a bit of hurry. I think Andrew and

佩琪：是啊，他們是很急，我覺得安德魯和克萊夫也可

Clive are ok. How soon can they get here?

以，他們最快什麼時候可以到？

Dexter: Andrew will be finishing his project in Korea at the end of next week. I can arrange for them to arrive in Taipei on 5th of April.

戴斯特：安德魯下星期就會把韓國的案子做完，我可以安排他們四月五日抵達台北。

Peggy: Well, it is a public holiday here. Would you be able to change it to April 6th?

佩琪：可是那天是國定假日，不然如果日期改到四月六日如何呢？

1 新多益基礎對話演練

2 新多益單篇對話和解析

3 新多益對話模擬試題

UNIT ③⓪

詢問工程師行程表

▶▶ 「短對話」填空練習 🎧 MP3 030

　　利用短對話強化聽力字彙以及拼字能力，答案的話請參照前面的對話喔！

Peggy: So do you know which _____ will be coming to do the _____ yet?

佩琪：那你知道是哪幾個工程師會來安裝了嗎？

Dexter: Well, at the moment I got Andrew and Clive available, I know you prefer _____, but he won't be available until the end of _____. I don't think the _____ can wait that long.

戴斯特：嗯，目前只有安德路還有克萊夫有空，我知道你比較想要馬克去，可是他要到五月底才會有空。我不認為客戶能夠等這麼久。

Peggy: Yes, they are in a bit of hurry. I think Andrew and Clive

佩琪：是啊，他們是很急，我覺得安德魯和克萊夫也可

are ok. How soon can they get here?

以，他們最快什麼時候可以到？

Dexter: Andrew will be finishing his _____ at the end of next week. I can arrange for them to arrive in _____ on _____ .

戴斯特：安德魯下星期就會把韓國的案子做完，我可以安排他們四月五日抵達台北。

Peggy: Well, it is a _____ here. Would you be able to change it to _____ ?

佩琪：可是那天是國定假日，不然如果日期改到四月六日如何呢？

UNIT 31

零件延誤

　　跟著短對話進行跟讀練習和覆誦，強化聽力專注力，現在就一起動身，開始聽「**短對話**」！

Peggy: Did Dexter mention that other than the standard installation, we also need to replace the filter system?

佩琪：戴斯特有跟你提過除了標準的安裝工作之外，還要更換原來的過濾設備嗎？

Andrew: Yes, he did.

安德魯：有，他有提到。

Peggy: But there is a slight delay with the filter system parts. They got stuck in customs and will probably take a few more days before they are released to us. Do you think you can start on the in-

佩琪：可是過濾設備的零件有點延誤，目前卡在海關，可能還要好幾天才會發回給我們。你可以先著手開始安裝工作然後晚一點再做過濾設備嗎？

stallation first and do the filter system later?

Andrew: I would prefer to do the filter system first, but I guess there is no other way. I just can't sit around and do nothing.

Peggy: Phew, thanks for that. I will be in so much trouble if you need those parts right away.

安德魯：我是希望先做過濾設備，可是現在也沒辦法，我總不能在這裡乾等。

佩琪：喔～你真是救星！如果你堅持要先做過濾設備的話那我就慘了。

零件延誤

▶▶ 「短對話」填空練習 🎧 MP3 031

利用短對話強化聽力字彙以及拼字能力，答案的話請參照前面的對話喔！

Peggy: Did Dexter mention that other than the _____, we also need to replace the _____?

佩琪：戴斯特有跟你提過除了標準的安裝工作之外，還要更換原來的過濾設備嗎？

Andrew: Yes, he did.

安德魯：有，他有提到。

Peggy: But there is a slight _____ with the filter system parts. They got stuck in _____ and will probably take a few more days before they are _____ to us. Do you think you can start on

佩琪：可是過濾設備的零件有點延誤，目前卡在海關，可能還要好幾天才會發回給我們。你可以先著手開始安裝工作然後晚一點再做過濾設備嗎？

the installation first and do the filter system later?

Andrew: I would prefer to do the filter system first, but I guess there is no other way. I just can't _____ and do nothing.

安德魯：我是希望先做過濾設備，可是現在也沒辦法，我總不能在這裡乾等。

Peggy: Phew, thanks for that. I will be in so much _____ if you need those parts right away.

佩琪：喔～你真是救星！如果你堅持要先做過濾設備的話那我就慘了。

對工程師的提點

▶▶ 影子跟讀「短對話」練習 🎧 MP3 032

　　跟著短對話進行跟讀練習和覆誦，強化聽力專注力，現在就一起動身，開始聽「**短對話**」！

Peggy: Since this is the first time, you work in this factory, there is something you need to know. There is a daily report that you need to fill out at the end of the day and make sure you get the department supervisor to sign it as well.

佩琪：既然這是你第一次到廠房做安裝，有些事情我需要跟你說明。下班前記得要填寫每日施工進度報告，還記得給部門主管簽名。

Andrew: Okay, which one is the department supervisor?

安德魯：好的，那主管是哪一個？

Peggy: It is Mr. Kao. The skin-

佩琪：是高先生，就是那個

ny guy with glasses. He normally does the morning shift and finishes work around 3 pm. The best time to catch him will be around lunch.

瘦瘦戴眼鏡的那一個。他通常是輪早班,所以三點就下班了。最容易找到他的時間就是午餐時間。

Andrew: Sure, anything else I need to know?

安德魯:好的,還有什麼是我需要注意的嗎?

Peggy: If you need any small parts, just go to the Maintenance Department. They will be happy to assist you.

佩琪:如果你需要一些小零件,那就直接去找維修部,他們很樂意提供。

對工程師的提點

▶▶ 「短對話」填空練習 🎧 MP3 032

利用短對話強化聽力字彙以及拼字能力，答案的話請參照前面的對話喔！

Peggy: Since this is the first time, you work in this _____ ____, there is something you need to know. There is a ____ _____ that you need to fill out at the end of the day and make sure you get the _____ ____ to sign it as well.

佩琪：既然這是你第一次到廠房做安裝，有些事情我需要跟你說明。下班前記得要填寫每日施工進度報告，還記得給部門主管簽名。

Andrew: Okay, which one is the department supervisor?

安德魯：好的，那主管是哪一個？

Peggy: It is Mr. Kao. The ____ _____ guy with _____.

佩琪：是高先生，就是那個瘦瘦戴眼鏡的那一個。他通

140

He normally does the _____ ____ and finishes work around 3 pm. The best time to catch him will be around lunch.

常是輪早班,所以三點就下班了。最容易找到他的時間就是午餐時間。

Andrew: Sure, anything else I need to know?

安德魯:好的,還有什麼是我需要注意的嗎?

Peggy: If you need any small parts, just go to the _____. They will be happy to assist you.

佩琪:如果你需要一些小零件,那就直接去找維修部,他們很樂意提供。

工程師反應問題

▶▶ 影子跟讀「短對話」練習 🎧 MP3 033

跟著短對話進行跟讀練習和覆誦，強化聽力專注力，現在就一起動身，開始聽「短對話」！

Andrew: Hello Peggy, I think the client will contact you shortly replacing an order for a set of parts. We are having a problem here. We discovered some of the electrical parts are worn out. We need to replace it; otherwise, it would not work properly.

安德魯：佩琪您好，客戶應該馬上會跟你聯絡要訂一組零件，我們安裝上有些問題，我們發現有些電路零件已經都磨損了，那些一訂要換，不然機器會出問題。

Peggy: Right. Do you have the part numbers? I can check whether the parts are in stock. If not, I will put in an urgent order for them.

佩琪：好的，那你有零件號碼嗎？我可以查一下有沒有庫存，如果沒有我就趕快下個緊急訂單。

Andrew: Sure, it is FE104-12 and two other cables. I also had them written down and gave it to the installation supervisor.

安德魯：有，那是FE104-12和其他兩組接線，我也有把號碼寫下來，已經拿給安裝負責人了。

Peggy: Thanks for the heads up, I will put the order through once I hear from them.

佩琪：謝謝你先告訴我，他們跟我聯絡之後我會馬上下訂單。

工程師反應問題

　　利用短對話強化聽力字彙以及拼字能力，答案的話請參照前面的對話喔！

Andrew: Hello Peggy, I think the ＿＿＿＿＿ will contact you shortly replacing an ＿＿＿＿＿ for a set of parts. We are having a problem here. We discovered some of the ＿＿＿＿＿ are worn out. We need to replace them; otherwise, it would not work properly.

安德魯：佩琪您好，客戶應該馬上會跟你聯絡要訂一組零件，我們安裝上有些問題，我們發現有些電路零件已經都磨損了，那些一訂要換，不然機器會出問題。

Peggy: Right. Do you have the part numbers? I can check whether the parts are ＿＿＿＿＿. If not, I will put in

佩琪：好的，那你有零件號碼嗎？我可以查一下有沒有庫存，如果沒有我就趕快下個緊急訂單。

an _____ for them.

Andrew: Sure, it is _____ and two other _____. I also had them written down and gave it to the installation supervisor.

Peggy: Thanks for the heads up, I will put the order through once I heard from them.

安德魯： 有，那是FE104-12和其他兩組接線，我也有把號碼寫下來，已經拿給安裝負責人了。

佩琪： 謝謝你先告訴我，他們跟我聯絡之後我會馬上下訂單。

準備試車／驗收

跟著短對話進行跟讀練習和覆誦，強化聽力專注力，現在就一起動身，開始聽「**短對話**」！

Peggy: Hi Andrew. How is the installation going? Do you think we will be ready for the commissioning?

佩琪：嗨，安德魯，安裝一切都順利嗎？你覺得下禮拜可以準備試車了嗎？

Andrew: I think the installation is going well, but there is a small hiccup that needs to be fixed with the feeding system. We will do the commissioning in a couple of days, and if all works out, we will be ready for the final test run next week.

安德魯：我認為安裝蠻順利的，只是送料系統還有些問題需要調整一下，我們兩天後會先試車，下禮拜就可以正式做驗收測試了。

Peggy: That's good to know. Let me know how you go with the test run because Mr. Chou would like to just be there for the final test run. I will organize for him to be there next week if all goes to plan.

佩琪：那太棒了！等試車完畢時麻煩你通知我一下，因為驗收測試的期間周先生想親自到場，如果一切順利的話，我就安排他下星期過去。

1 新多益基礎對話演練

2 新多益單篇對話和解析

3 新多益對話模擬試題

準備試車／驗收

▶▶ 「短對話」填空練習 🎧 MP3 034

利用短對話強化聽力字彙以及拼字能力，答案的話請參照前面的對話喔！

Peggy: Hi Andrew. How is the _____ going? Do you think we will be ready for the _____?

佩琪：嗨，安德魯，安裝一切都順利嗎？你覺得下禮拜可以準備試車了嗎？

Andrew: I think the installation is going well, but there is a _____ that needs to be _____ with the feeding system. We will do the commissioning in a couple of days, and if all works out, we will be ready for the _____ run next week.

安德魯：我認為安裝蠻順利的，只是送料系統還有些問題需要調整一下，我們兩天後會先試車，下禮拜就可以正式做驗收測試了。

Peggy: That's good to know. Let me know how you go with the test run because Mr. Chou would like to be there for the final test run. I will _____ for him to just be there _____ ____ if all goes to plan.

佩琪：那太棒了！等試車完畢時麻煩你通知我一下，因為驗收測試的期間周先生想親自到場，如果一切順利的話，我就安排他下星期過去。

通知供應廠已順利完工

▶ **影子跟讀「短對話」練習** 🎧 MP3 035

　　跟著短對話進行跟讀練習和覆誦，強化聽力專注力，現在就一起動身，開始聽**「短對話」**！

Peggy: Hi Dexter. Good news for you. The installation is all sorted out and the commissioning and the final acceptance run both went well. We are in the process of getting the paperwork done. The end user will sign the certificate of acceptance shortly.

佩琪：戴斯特您好，有個好消息跟你說，安裝已經完成了，試車還有驗收測試都很順利，我們目前正在處理相關的文件作業，客戶很快就會簽驗收證書了。以離開？他們兩星期後還有其他的安裝工作要做。

Dexter: That's wonderful. So when do you think I can have the engineers back? They got another project to attend to

戴斯特：那太好了，那工程師甚麼時候可以離開？他們兩星期後還有其他的安裝工作要做。

in two weeks time.

Peggy: Well, they need to stay on for one more week to complete the staff training. If you need them back right after that, then you can arrange for them to fly out either next Friday night or Saturday morning.

佩琪：這樣啊，他們還需要多留一個星期來做員工訓練，如果你很急著要他們回去，那就安排下星期五晚上或是星期六早上回去好了。

1 新多益基礎對話演練

2 新多益單篇對話和解析

3 新多益對話模擬試題

通知供應廠已順利完工

▶▶「短對話」填空練習　🎧 MP3 035

利用短對話強化聽力字彙以及拼字能力，答案的話請參照前面的對話喔！

Peggy: Hi Dexter. Good news for you. The installation is all sorted out and the commissioning and the _____ run both went well. We are in the _____ of getting the _____ done. The end user will sign the _____ of acceptance shortly.

佩琪： 戴斯特您好，有個好消息跟你說，安裝已經完成了，試車還有驗收測試都很順利，我們目前正在處理相關的文件作業，客戶很快就會簽驗收證書了。以離開？他們兩星期後還有其他的安裝工作要做。

Dexter: That's wonderful. So when do you think I can have the _____ back? They got another _____ to attend to in _____ time.

戴斯特： 那太好了，那工程師甚麼時候可以離開？他們兩星期後還有其他的安裝工作要做。

Peggy: Well, they need to stay on for one more week to complete the _____. If you need them back right after that, then you can _____ _____ for them to fly out either _____ night or _____ _____.

佩琪：這樣啊，他們還需要多留一個星期來做員工訓練，如果你很急著要他們回去，那就安排下星期五晚上或是星期六早上回去好了。

日本奈良：鹿的粉紅迷戀和photo credit

▶▶ 影子跟讀「短對話」練習 🎧 MP3 036

　　跟著短對話進行跟讀練習和覆誦，強化聽力專注力，現在就一起動身，開始聽「**短對話**」！

Mary: I do think they're gonna be so impressed... those couple of frames looks stunning.

瑪莉：我真的認為他們會對此留下深刻印象...那幾張照片看起來很美。

Cindy: Thanks... you know something about "photo credit"? It really belongs to the photographer, capturing a really fine moment of me. Plus, Nara looks so beautiful.

辛蒂：謝謝...你知道有關於「照片來源」嗎？這真的要歸功於攝影師，捕捉到我真的很美的時刻。再者，奈良看起來真的很美。

Chris: My pleasure... Ouch!

克里斯：我的榮幸...哎喲！

Cindy: What's going on?

辛蒂：發生什麼事了？

Chris: he bit me. Oh my butt... that hurts.

克里斯：他咬我。嘔我的屁股…真的痛。

Mary: that deer...? Too hilarious... I told you not to wear pink. Perhaps he has some obsessions or fantasy about pink... or maybe he happens not to be a vegetarian.

瑪莉：那隻鹿…嗎？太好笑了吧…我早告訴你別穿粉紅色了。或許他對粉紅色有著迷戀或幻想…或是或許他可能剛好不是素食者。

Cindy: if the editor-in-chief were here, she would be laughed out of the room.

辛蒂：如果總編在這的話，她會笑掉牙吧。

日本奈良：鹿的粉紅迷戀和photo credit

▶▶ 「短對話」填空練習 🎧 MP3 036

　　利用短對話強化聽力字彙以及拼字能力，答案的話請參照前面的對話喔！

Mary: I do think they're gonna be so _____... those couple of _____ looks __ _____.

瑪莉：我真的認為他們會對此留下深刻印象...那幾張照片看起來很美。

Cindy: Thanks... you know something about "photo credit"? It really belongs to the _____, _____ a really fine _____ of me. Plus, Nara looks so _____.

辛蒂：謝謝...你知道有關於「照片來源」嗎？這真的要歸功於攝影師，捕捉到我真的很美的時刻。再者，奈良看起來真的很美。

Chris: My pleasure... Ouch!

克里斯：我的榮幸...哎喲！

Cindy: What's going on?

辛蒂：發生什麼事了？

Chris: he bit me. Oh my ____ _____... that hurts.

克里斯：他咬我。嘔我的屁股…真的痛。

Mary: that deer...? Too ____ _____... I told you not to ____ _____. Perhaps he has some _____ o r _____ about pink... or maybe he happens not to be a _____ __.

瑪莉：那隻鹿…嗎？太好笑了吧…我早告訴你別穿粉紅色了。或許他對粉紅色有著迷戀或幻想…或是或許他可能剛好不是素食者。

Cindy: if the editor-in-chief were here, she would be __ _____ out of the room.

辛蒂：如果總編在這的話，她會笑掉牙吧。

尋找精子捐贈者：...可是最優質的居然要等到2025年了

▶▶ 影子跟讀「短對話」練習　🎧 MP3 037

跟著短對話進行跟讀練習和覆誦，強化聽力專注力，現在就一起動身，開始聽「短對話」！

Jack: I've narrowed the donors down to four candidates. If you still can't pick one, then my hands are tied.

傑克：我已經把人選縮小到剩四個了。如果你仍選不出來，那我真的束手無策了。

Mary: it's really hard to decide. They seem so perfect.

瑪莉：真的很難決定。他們似乎都很完美。

Linda: picking the right sperm donor is harder than I thought. BY-1007 is married.

琳達：選個合適的精子捐贈者比我想像中難多了。BY-1007結婚了。

Mary: what about BF-1007? He's handsome and he has a master's degree from Harvard.

瑪莉：那BF-1007呢？他英俊且他有哈佛的碩士學位。

Linda: they all graduated from Ivy League schools. I do need to look at other criteria.

Mary: CF-1006. He is a model... OMG he is in the oatmeal commercial.

Linda: but he is 35 years old.

Mary: CY-1007. He is a pilot and an athlete.

Linda: OMG he is perfect. That guy for the sperm donor ad campaign.

Jack: Oh... him... but he won't be available until 2025. I guess someone's egg can't wait that long.

琳達：他們都從常春藤盟校畢業。我想我需要看其他的條件。

瑪莉：CF-1006。他是模特兒...天啊他是燕麥粥廣告的那個人。

琳達：可是他35歲了。

瑪莉：CY-1007。他是飛行員也是運動員。

琳達：天啊他很完美。那個精子捐贈者廣告宣傳的那個男的。

傑克：喔...他...但是他在2025年前都沒空。我想有人的卵子可能等不了這麼久。

尋找精子捐贈者：...可是最優質的居然要等到2025年了

▶▶「短對話」填空練習 🎧 MP3 037

利用短對話強化聽力字彙以及拼字能力，答案的話請參照前面的對話喔！

Jack: I've _____ the _____ _____ down to four _____ __. If you still can't pick one, then my hands _____.

傑克：我已經把人選縮小到剩四個了。如果你仍選不出來，那我真的束手無策了。

Mary: it's really hard to decide. They seem so _____ __.

瑪莉：真的很難決定。他們似乎都很完美。

Linda: picking the right sperm donor is harder than I thought. BY-1007 is _____ __.

琳達：選個合適的精子捐贈者比我想像中難多了。BY-1007結婚了。

Mary: what about BF-1007? He's _____ and he has a

瑪莉：那BF-1007呢？他英俊且他有哈佛的碩士學位。

master's degree from _____ ___.

Linda: they all graduated from Ivy _____ schools. I do need to look at other ___ _____.

琳達：他們都從常春藤盟校畢業。我想我需要看其他的條件。

Mary: CF-1006. He is a _____ ___... OMG he is in the ___ _____ _____.

瑪莉：CF-1006。他是模特兒...天啊他是燕麥粥廣告的那個人。

Linda: but he is 35 years old.

琳達：可是他35歲了。

Mary: CY-1007. He is a _____ ___ and an _____.

瑪莉：CY-1007。他是飛行員也是運動員。

Linda: OMG he is perfect. That guy for the _____ donor ad _____.

琳達：天啊他很完美。那個精子捐贈者廣告宣傳的那個男的。

Jack: Oh... him... but he won't be _____ until 2025. I guess someone's egg can't wait that long.

傑克：喔...他...但是他在2025年前都沒空。我想有人的卵子可能等不了這麼久。

球星簽約：跳脫框架思考就能在法律規範下也簽成功高檔球星

▶▶ 影子跟讀「短對話」練習 🎧 MP3 038

跟著短對話進行跟讀練習和覆誦，強化聽力專注力，現在就一起動身，開始聽**「短對話」**！

Chris: we have to sign two potential basketball stars on a very tight budget. And there is no way that we can sign Derek under the law. He wants 10 million dollars, not 8.

克里斯：我們必需以非常緊縮的預算簽兩個有潛力的籃球球星。根據現在法條的規定我們不可能簽下德瑞克。他想要1千萬美元，而不是8百萬美元。

Jimmy: that's right. Legitimately, we can only sign him at 8 million dollars, but we can still get him… we just have to think outside the box.

吉米：對的。法律上我們只能夠以8百萬美元簽下他，但是我們仍可以簽下他…我們只是需要跳出框架思考。

Chris: how? Bribe him?

克里斯：如何？賄絡他嗎？

Jimmy: absolutely not... we can sign Jack but cut his pay from 7 million dollars to 5, and we can assure Derek that we're going to pay him the extra 2 in private. It's in cash... no one knows.

Chris: brilliant... but how to persuade Jack to sign at 5 million dollars.

Jimmy: invite him to the dinner, making him look like a big shot or something.

Chris: problem solved.

吉米：當然不是...我們可以簽下傑克但是將他的費用從7百萬美元砍到5百萬美元，而且我們可以向德瑞克保證我們會私底下付他另外的兩百萬美元。是付現...沒有人會知道。

克里斯：真高明...但是要如何說服傑克以5百萬美元簽下呢？

吉米：邀請他來晚餐，服侍他讓他像個大咖或什麼的。

克里斯：問題解決了。

球星簽約：跳脫框架思考就能在法律規範下也簽成功高檔球星

▶▶「短對話」填空練習 🎧 MP3 038

　　利用短對話強化聽力字彙以及拼字能力，答案的話請參照前面的對話喔！

Chris: we have to _____ two _____ _____ stars on a very tight _____. And there is no way that we can sign Derek under the _____. He wants 10 million dollars, not 8.

克里斯：我們必需以非常緊縮的預算簽兩個有潛力的籃球球星。根據現在法條的規定我們不可能簽下德瑞克。他想要1千萬美元，而不是8百萬美元。

Jimmy: that's right. _____, we can only sign him at 8 million dollars, but we can still get him... we just have to think _____ the box.

吉米：對的。法律上我們只能夠以8百萬美元簽下他，但是我們仍可以簽下他…我們只是需要跳出框架思考。

Chris: how? Bribe him?

克里斯：如何？賄絡他嗎？

Jimmy: _____ not... we can sign Jack but cut his pay from 7 million dollars to 5, and we can _____ Derek that we're going to pay him the _____ 2 in private. It's in cash... no one knows.

Chris: _____... but how to _____ Jack to sign at 5 million dollars.

Jimmy: invite him to the dinner, making him look like a _____ or something.

Chris: problem solved.

吉米：當然不是...我們可以簽下傑克但是將他的費用從7百萬美元砍到5百萬美元，而且我們可以向德瑞克保證我們會私底下付他另外的兩百萬美元。是付現...沒有人會知道。

克里斯：真高明...但是要如何說服傑克以5百萬美元簽下呢？

吉米：邀請他來晚餐，服侍他讓他像個大咖或什麼的。

克里斯：問題解決了。

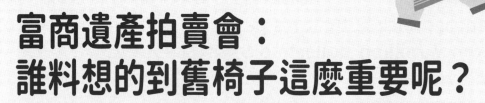

UNIT ❸❾

富商遺產拍賣會：
誰料想的到舊椅子這麼重要呢？

▶▶ 影子跟讀「短對話」練習　🎧 MP3 039

　　跟著短對話進行跟讀練習和覆誦，強化聽力專注力，現在就一起動身，開始聽「**短對話**」！

Nick: this is not the annual auction. We're here on behalf of the owner of antique shop and hotel chains to arrange this auction... and announce Rick Chen's will...his money will be given to five kids evenly. So today we will auction something in his office and other things.

Jack: Old chair... are you kidding me...

尼克：這不是年度拍賣。我們代表古董店和旅館連鎖店的擁有者安排這個銷售會...和宣布瑞克陳的遺囑...他的金錢將會平均分配給五個孩子。所以今天我們會拍賣他辦公室的東西和其他東西。

傑克：舊椅子...你在跟我開玩笑嗎...

Linda: why didn't dad just give us these paintings... I don't have that much money in my bank account let alone buying them.

琳達：為什麼老爸就不給我們那些畫呢...我銀行存款也沒有那個多現金，更別說要購買了。

Nick: old chair for 500 dollars...ok... old chair for 300 dollars... do any of the family members want a chair for 300 dollars. The chair actually represents your father... Since there is none... the auction is over. All his shares of hotel chains and listed items will be donated to charity... thank you guys.

尼克：舊椅子五百美元...好的...舊椅子300美元...有任何家庭成員想要以300美元購買椅子嗎？這椅子實際上代表著你的父親...既然沒有的話...這個拍賣會結束了。所有他的旅館連店股份和列表的項目都會捐贈給慈善機構...謝謝各位。

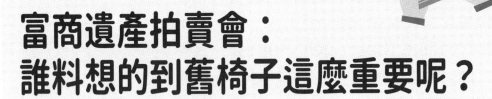

富商遺產拍賣會：
誰料想的到舊椅子這麼重要呢？

▶▶ 「短對話」填空練習　🎧 MP3 039

利用短對話強化聽力字彙以及拼字能力，答案的話請參照前面的對話喔！

Nick: this is not the _____ __ auction. We're here on __ _____ of the owner of ____ _____ shop and hotel chains to _____ this auction... and _____ Rick Chen's will...his money will be given to five kids _____. So to-day we will auction something in his office and other things.

尼克：這不是年度拍賣。我們代表古董店和旅館連鎖店的擁有者安排這個銷售會...和宣布瑞克陳的遺囑...他的金錢將會平均分配給五個孩子。所以今天我們會拍賣他辦公室的東西和其他東西。

Jack: _____ ... are you kidding me...

傑克：舊椅子...你在跟我開玩笑嗎...

Linda: why didn't dad just give us these _____ ... I don't have that much money in my bank _____ let alone buying them.

琳達：為什麼老爸就不給我們那些畫呢...我銀行存款也沒有那個多現金，更別説要購買了。

Nick: old chair for 500 dollars...ok... old chair for 300 dollars... do any of the family _____ want a chair for 300 dollars. The chair actually _____ your father... Since there is none... the auction is over. All his shares of hotel chains and _____ __ will be _____ to charity... thank you guys.

尼克：舊椅子五百美元...好的...舊椅子300美元...有任何家庭成員想要以300美元購買椅子嗎？這椅子實際上代表著你的父親...既然沒有的話...這個拍賣會結束了。所有他的旅館連店股份和列表的項目都會捐贈給慈善機構...謝謝各位。

討論加班：工作狂就是希望有多些overtime啊!

跟著短對話進行跟讀練習和覆誦，強化聽力專注力，現在就一起動身，開始聽**「短對話」**！

Cindy: why do people complain about overtime? I'm begging for more. I need lots of money.

辛蒂：為什麼人們都抱怨加班呢？我還乞求更多。我需要更多的錢。

Jack: only to you... you're such a... workaholic.

傑克：只有你這樣想吧…你真是個…工作狂。

Mary: since there is a hiring freeze and a lack of orders... I don't think your overtime dream is gonna come true.

瑪莉：既然有雇用冷凍期和缺乏訂單…我不覺得你的加班夢會成真。

Cindy: too bad... I guess I will just sell some home-baked cookies during the week-ends.

辛蒂：真不巧…那我只好在週末時販賣一些家庭烘培餅乾。

Jack: I'm missing the chocolate chips with hazelnuts.

傑克：我還真想唸有著榛子的巧克力餅乾。

Mary: just a perfect blend with coffee. Perhaps you can make some serious money by opening your own shop someday.

瑪莉：搭咖啡真的是完美的組合。或許你可以真的賺進一筆錢，有天開了你自己的店。

討論加班：工作狂就是希望有多些overtime啊！

▶ 「短對話」填空練習 🎧 MP3 040

利用短對話強化聽力字彙以及拼字能力，答案的話請參照前面的對話喔！

Cindy: why do people _____ ____ about _____? I'm begging for more. I need lots of _____.

辛蒂：為什麼人們都抱怨加班呢？我還乞求更多。我需要更多的錢。

Jack: only to you... you're such a... _____.

傑克：只有你這樣想吧...你真是個...工作狂。

Mary: since there is a _____ ____ _____ and a lack of orders... I don't think your overtime dream is gonna come true.

瑪莉：既然有雇用冷凍期和缺乏訂單...我不覺得你的加班夢會成真。

Cindy: too bad... I guess I will just sell some _____ cookies during the _____.

辛蒂：真不巧...那我只好在週末時販賣一些家庭烘培餅乾。

Jack: I'm missing the _____ chips with _____.

傑克：我還真想唸有著榛子的巧克力餅乾。

Mary: just a perfect _____ with _____. Perhaps you can make some _____ money by opening your own _____ someday.

瑪莉：搭咖啡真的是完美的組合。或許你可以真的賺進一筆錢，有天開了你自己的店。

1 新多益基礎對話演練

2 新多益單篇對話和解析

3 新多益對話模擬試題

史丹佛的分類：
你是techie還是fussy呢？

▶▶ 影子跟讀「短對話」練習　🎧 MP3 041

跟著短對話進行跟讀練習和覆誦，強化聽力專注力，現在就一起動身，開始聽「**短對話**」！

Jack: Relax... they're in a meeting. So are you a techie or a fuzzy?

傑克：放輕鬆…他們在開會。所以你是科技人還是社科人呢？

Cindy: what do you mean?

辛蒂：你指的是什麼呢？

Jack: the fuzzies refer to students of the humanities and social sciences, whereas the techies refer to students of the engineering or hard science. It's a categorization from Stanford.

傑克：模糊性指的是人文社會科學學系的學生，而技術專家指的是工程或純科學學系的學生。這是史丹佛的分類。

Cindy: I see... then I'm a techie... I majored in Chemistry.

辛蒂：我懂了...那麼我是技術專家...我主修是化學。

Jack: I prefer to call myself a techie... but I'm actually a fuzzy... it's funnier. What about you husband?

傑克：我偏好將自己稱作技術專家...但我實際上是人文社會科學學系學生...只是有趣些。那你丈夫呢？

Cindy: a fuzzy. He was a Chinese major.

辛蒂：人文社會科學學系學生。他是中文系主修。

Jack: You guys complement each other. Normally a fuzzy dates a techie... that's how things normally go.

傑克：你們真的彼此互補。通常人文科系學生跟理工科系學生約會...事情通常都是這樣走。

1 新多益基礎對話演練

2 新多益單篇對話和解析

3 新多益對話模擬試題

史丹佛的分類：
你是techie還是fussy呢？

　　利用短對話強化聽力字彙以及拼字能力，答案的話請參照前面的對話喔！

Jack: Relax... they're in a _____ _____. So are you a _____ __ or a _____?

傑克：放輕鬆...他們在開會。所以你是科技人還是社科人呢？

Cindy: what do you mean?

辛蒂：你指的是什麼呢？

Jack: the fuzzies refer to students of the _____ and _____ sciences, whereas the techies refer to students of the _____ or _____ __ science. It's a _____ from _____.

傑克：模糊性指的是人文社會科學學系的學生，而技術專家指的是工程或純科學學系的學生。這是史丹佛的分類。

Cindy: I see... then I'm a te-chie... I majored in _____.

辛蒂：我懂了...那麼我是技術專家...我主修是化學。

Jack: I prefer to call myself a techie... but I'm actually a fuzzy... it's _____. What about you _____?

傑克：我偏好將自己稱作技術專家...但我實際上是人文社會科學學系學生...只是有趣些。那你丈夫呢？

Cindy: a fuzzy. He was a ____ _____ major.

辛蒂：人文社會科學學系學生。他是中文系主修。

Jack: You guys _____ each other. Normally a fuzzy dates a _____... that's how things _____ go.

傑克：你們真的彼此互補。通常人文科系學生跟理工科系學生約會...事情通常都是這樣走。

總機代接：
藥品的銷售業務代表致電

跟著短對話進行跟讀練習和覆誦，強化聽力專注力，現在就一起動身，開始聽「**短對話**」！

Mary: how may I direct your call?

瑪莉：我要幫您轉接給誰呢？

Jack: this is Jack Collins... a sales rep of Best pharmaceuticals... is Linda available? I'd like to discuss the orders with her. There seems to be a terrible misunderstanding.

傑克：這是傑克·柯林斯...倍斯特藥品的銷售業務代表...琳達目前有空嗎？我想與她討論關於訂單的事。似乎有個嚴重的誤會。

Mary: I see... but she is having a business meeting in Paris. Or do you wanna to talk to the other sales reps...

瑪莉：我懂了...但是她正在巴黎開商務會議。或是你可以跟其他銷售代表談談...我可以替您轉接電話。

I can direct the call for you.

Jack: No thanks... when will she be back from the trip?

傑克：不，謝謝...她什麼時候會回來呢？

Mary: July 14, 2018...

瑪莉：2018年7月14日...

Jack: I think I can call back later... thanks again.

傑克：我想我可以稍後再撥...謝謝了。

1 新多益基礎對話演練

2 新多益單篇對話和解析

3 新多益對話模擬試題

總機代接：
藥品的銷售業務代表致電

▶▶ 「短對話」填空練習　🎧 MP3 042

　　利用短對話強化聽力字彙以及拼字能力，答案的話請參照前面的對話喔！

Mary: how may I _____ your call?

瑪莉：我要幫您轉接給誰呢？

Jack: this is Jack Collins... a sales rep of Best _____... is Linda _____? I'd like to _____ the orders with her. There seems to be a terrible _____.

傑克：這是傑克·柯林斯...倍斯特藥品的銷售業務代表...琳達目前有空嗎？我想與她討論關於訂單的事。似乎有個嚴重的誤會。

Mary: I see... but she is having a _____ meeting in __ _____. Or do you wanna to talk to the other _____...

瑪莉：我懂了...但是她正在巴黎開商務會議。或是你可以跟其他銷售代表談談...我可以替您轉接電話。

I can _____ the call for you.

Jack: No thanks... when will she be _____ from the __ _____?

傑克：不，謝謝...她什麼時候會回來呢？

Mary: July 14, 2018...

瑪莉：2018年7月14日...

Jack: I think I can _____ later... thanks again.

傑克：我想我可以稍後再撥...謝謝了。

1 新多益基礎對話演練

2 新多益單篇對話和解析

3 新多益對話模擬試題

倍斯特巧克力工廠❶：巧克力嚐到不想再嚐了！

▶▶ 影子跟讀「短對話」練習 🎧 MP3 043

跟著短對話進行跟讀練習和覆誦，強化聽力專注力，現在就一起動身，開始聽「**短對話**」！

Manager: ...ok... now dig in...	經理：...好的...現在大口品嚐...。
Employee: that many...?	員工：...這麼多呀...?
Manager: ...is that a problem? ...you guys are hired to taste chocolates... so open your mouth and have a big bite...	經理：...這樣有什麼問題嗎? ...你們是受聘要品嚐巧克力味道的...所以打開你的嘴巴並且大口吃下...。
Employee: ...ok... I'm gonna get some drinks from the automatic machine...I'm so thirty...	員工：...好的...我想要從自動販賣機那裡投遞些飲料...我好渴...。

Manager: ...you guys are grown-ups... why ask my permission?? Go... I will be right back in twenty minutes... and by that time I want to know how each new flavor tastes like... ok... great...

Employee❷: ...now whenever I go to the store... my fantasy for the chocolate is gone...

Employee: ...can't agree with you more... but I've got to say that this one does stand out from the rest...it's unconventional...

Employee❷: ...perhaps I should've tried that one first...

經理：...你們都是成年人了...為什麼需要我批准呢？去吧...我20分鐘後會回來這裡...然後到那時候，我想要知道每個口味嚐起來是怎樣...好的...很棒...。

員工❷：...現在不論我走到哪間店...我對巧克力的幻想全都沒了...。

員工：...不能同意你更多了...但是我必須説，巧克力口味是鶴立雞群的...這是非常規的...。

員工❷：...或許我應該要先試試看這個...。

倍斯特巧克力工廠❶：巧克力嚐到不想再嚐了！

▶▶ 「短對話」填空練習 🎧 MP3 043

　　利用短對話強化聽力字彙以及拼字能力，答案的話請參照前面的對話喔！

Manager: ...ok... now _____ _____...

經理：...好的...現在大口品嚐...。

Employee: that many...?

員工：...這麼多呀...?

Manager: ...is that a _____ __? ...you guys are _____ to _____ chocolates... so open your _____ and have a big _____...

經理：...這樣有什麼問題嗎？...你們是受聘要品嚐巧克力味道的...所以打開你的嘴巴並且大口吃下...。

Employee: ...ok... I'm gonna get some drinks from the _____ machine...I'm so __ _____...

員工：...好的...我想要從自動販賣機那裡投遞些飲料...我好渴...。

Manager: ...you guys are __ _____... why ask my _____ ____?? Go... I will be right back in _____ minutes... and by that time I want to know how each new _____ __ tastes like... ok... great...

Employee❷: ...now _____ __ I go to the store... my ____ _____ for the chocolate is __ _____...

Employee: ...can't agree with you more... but I've got to say that this one does _____ ____ from the rest...it's _____ ____...

Employee❷: ..._____ I should've tried that one first...

經理：...你們都是成年人了...為什麼需要我批准呢？去吧...我20分鐘後會回來這裡...然後到那時候，我想要知道每個口味嚐起來是怎樣...好的...很棒...。

員工❷：...現在不論我走到哪間店...我對巧克力的幻想全都沒了...。

員工：...不能同意你更多了...但是我必須要說，巧克力口味是鶴立雞群的...這是非常規的...。

員工❷：...或許我應該要先試試看這個...。

倍斯特巧克力工廠❷：開會時最好還是提個問題吧！

▶▶ 影子跟讀「短對話」練習　🎧 MP3 044

　　跟著短對話進行跟讀練習和覆誦，強化聽力專注力，現在就一起動身，開始聽「**短對話**」！

Manager: ...I've seen the questionnaires you guys filled... it's ok... I won't judge... I want the honest opinion... to see if there's room for improvement... and I'm giving the feedback to the lab... are there any questions?

Employee: ...if there is none...he is gonna be so furious... (lower the voice)

Employee❷: ...sorry... I have one...

經理：...我已經看過你們填的問卷了...這是OK的...我不會評論...我想要最真實的意見...去看是否還有進步的空間呢...而且我會將回饋的建議交給實驗室...還有什麼問題嗎？

員工：...如果沒有問題的話...他又要很憤怒了...（降低音量）

員工❷：...抱歉...我有一個問題...。

Manager: ...shoot... why wait...? I'm dying to know...

經理：...快說...為何等待...?我超想知道...。

Employee❷: ...I do love the decorations for type A... and I was thinking something bolder... can it be made into a cartoon character or tailor-made and go with the modern sayings... some phrases that teenagers usually use...

員工❷：...我喜愛A類型的裝飾品...而且我曾思考著一些更大膽的想法...能夠製作成卡通的角色或是量身訂作以及搭配現代化俗諺的...有些諺語青少年常使用的...。

Manager: ...excellent... I think you've made a point... and I wanna you to go the lab with me and explain the concept to those lab researchers... and it's best if I don't get involved...otherwise... it's like an order... made by the boss...

經理：...很出色...我認為你已講到重點了...而我想要你跟我一起到實驗室去將這些概念解釋給實驗室的研究人員...而且最好的就是我沒有牽涉其中...否則...這會像是由老闆所發出的命令...。

倍斯特巧克力工廠❷：開會時最好還是提個問題吧！

▶▶ 「短對話」填空練習 🎧 MP3 044

利用短對話強化聽力字彙以及拼字能力，答案的話請參照前面的對話喔！

Manager: ...I've seen the _____ _____ you guys _____... it's ok... I won't judge... I want the _____ opinion... to see if there's _____ for _____... and I'm giving the feedback to the _____ ... are there any questions?

Employee: ...if there is none...he is gonna be so _____ _____... (lower the voice)

Employee❷: ...sorry... I have one...

經理：...我已經看過你們填的問卷了...這是OK的...我不會評論...我想要最真實的意見...去看是否還有進步的空間呢...而且我會將回饋的建議交給實驗室...還有什麼問題嗎？

員工：...如果沒有問題的話...他又要很憤怒了...（降低音量）

員工❷：...抱歉...我有一個問題...。

Manager: ...shoot... why wait...? I'm _____ know...

經理：...快説...為何等待...？我超想知道...。

Employee❷: ...I do love the _____ for type A... and I was thinking something ____ _____... can it be made into a _____ character or tailor-made and go with the __ _____ sayings... some ____ _____ that _____ usually use...

員工❷：...我喜愛A類型的裝飾品...而且我曾思考著一些更大膽的想法...能夠製作成卡通的角色或是量身訂作以及搭配現代化俗諺的...有些諺語青少年常使用的...。

Manager: ..._____... I think you've made a point... and I wanna you to go the lab with me and explain the _____ to those lab _____ ... and it's best if I don't get _____...otherwise... it's like an order... made by the boss...

經理：...很出色...我認為你已講到重點了...而我想要你跟我一起到實驗室去將這些概念解釋給實驗室的研究人員...而且最好的就是我沒有牽涉其中...否則...這會像是由老闆所發出的命令...。

倍斯特巧克力工廠❸：切蛋糕慶祝升遷

▶▶ 影子跟讀「短對話」練習 🎧 MP3 045

　　跟著短對話進行跟讀練習和覆誦，強化聽力專注力，現在就一起動身，開始聽「**短對話**」！

Manager: ...the chocolate that is adapted into the animal shape sold really well... I've got to say that Mary is a rising star... so I'm giving her a promotion... the head of the department... congratulations...

經理：...這巧克力改製成動物的形狀銷售的相當好...我必須要說的是瑪莉是顆看漲的星星...所以我要給她升遷...這個部門的首腦...恭喜...。

Employee❷: ...thanks... I'm honored... and I wanna say thanks to all colleagues in the department...

員工❷：...謝謝...我感到榮幸...而且我想要對所有部門的同事說謝謝...。

Manager: ...I'm gonna get the cake... you have to ex-

經理：...我去拿蛋糕...你們必須要見諒下，我要離開幾

cuse me for a few seconds..

Employee❷: ...I can't believe... it's so serendipitous...

Employee: ...that means more responsibility shouldering on you...

Employee❷: ...I guess... that means I have to be an early bird in the morning... I can't leave early and the frequent visit to the lab...

Employee: ...don't worry about it... you are gonna do the job just fine...

Manager: ...the cake is ready... let's cut the cake... congratulations...

Employee❷: ...thanks...

秒鐘...。

員工❷：...我不敢相信...這太奇緣了...。

員工：...這意謂著更多的責任加在你身上...。

員工❷：...我想...這意謂著，每天早晨我都要早到公司，我不會早走而且要更頻繁的往實驗室走...。

員工：...別擔心...做這份工作你沒問題的...。

經理：...蛋糕準備好了...我們來切蛋糕...恭喜...。

員工❷：...謝謝...。

倍斯特巧克力工廠❸：切蛋糕慶祝升遷

▶ 「短對話」填空練習　🎧 MP3 045

　　利用短對話強化聽力字彙以及拼字能力，答案的話請參照前面的對話喔！

Manager: ...the chocolate that is _____ into the _____ shape sold really well... I've got to say that Mary is a rising star... so I'm giving her a promotion... the head of the _____... congratulations...

經理：...這巧克力改製成動物的形狀銷售的相當好...我必須要說的是瑪莉是顆看漲的星星...所以我要給她升遷...這個部門的首腦...恭喜...。

Employee❷: ...thanks... I'm honored... and I wanna say thanks to all _____ in the department...

員工❷：...謝謝...我感到榮幸...而且我想要對所有部門的同事說謝謝...。

Manager: ...I'm gonna get _____ ... you have to

經理：...我去拿蛋糕...你們必須要見諒下，我要離開幾

_____ me for a few seconds..

秒鐘...。

Employee❷: ...I can't be-lieve... it's so _____...

員工❷：...我不敢相信...這太奇緣了...。

Employee: ...that means more _____ _____ on you...

員工：...這意謂著更多的責任加在你身上...。

Employee❷: ...I guess... that means I have to be an _____ in the morning... I can't _____ early and the _____ visit to the lab...

員工❷：...我想...這意謂著，每天早晨我都要早到公司，我不會早走而且要更頻繁的往實驗室走...。

Employee: ...don't worry about it... you are gonna do the job just fine...

員工：...別擔心...做這份工作你沒問題的...。

Manager: ...the cake is _____... let's cut the cake... _____...

經理：...蛋糕準備好了...我們來切蛋糕...恭喜...。

Employee❷: ...thanks...

員工❷：...謝謝...。

倍斯特巧克力工廠❹：
別困惑了，好好接受升遷喜悅吧！

▶▶ 影子跟讀「短對話」練習　🎧 MP3 046

　　跟著短對話進行跟讀練習和覆誦，強化聽力專注力，現在就一起動身，開始聽「短對話」！

Employee❷: ...I'm feeling a bit confused... about the promotion.

員工❷：...關於升遷的事情......我感到困惑

Manager: ...confused about what... tomorrow I'll have the HR personnel to give you a new card and a new ID badge... and you'll have your own office room

經理：...困惑什麼呢...明天我會要人事專員給你新的卡片和新的ID識別證...而且你會有你自己的辦公室。

Employee❷: ...this just happens so fast...

員工❷：...只是這一切發生的太快了...。

Manager: ...it's a rare opportunity... just embrace it...

經理：...這是罕見的機會...就接受它吧...。

Employee❷: ...tell me what the upside is... other than the office room...

員工❷：...告訴我優點是什麼...除了辦公室房間...。

Manager: ...there's going to be a 40% bump in your salary... I can't say that in public...

經理：...你的薪資會有40%的調漲...我無法在大庭廣眾下說...。

Employee❷: ...seriously...? ...wow...then I will take it... I'm thrilled...

員工❷：...真的嗎...? ...哇！...那麼我會接受它...我感到興奮...。

Manager: ...and you will have your own parking space...

經理：...而且你會有你自己的停車空位...。

Employee❷: ...terrific... now I'm feeling it... I eat my own way up to the position I'm in... I need more wine

員工❷：...太棒了...現在我感受到了...我靠吃爬升到我現在的位置上...我需要更多的酒...。

Manager: ... you surely are...

經理：...你確實需要...。

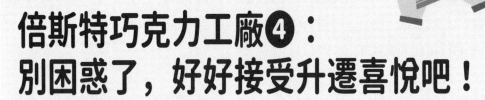

UNIT 46

倍斯特巧克力工廠❹：
別困惑了，好好接受升遷喜悅吧！

▶▶ 「短對話」填空練習 🎧 MP3 046

利用短對話強化聽力字彙以及拼字能力，答案的話請參照前面的對話喔！

Employee❷: ...I'm feeling a bit _____ ... about the __ _____.

員工❷：...關於升遷的事情......我感到困惑

Manager: ...confused about what... tomorrow I'll have the HR _____ to give you a new _____ and a new _____ ... and you'll have your own _____ room

經理：...困惑什麼呢...明天我會要人事專員給你新的卡片和新的ID識別證...而且你會有你自己的辦公室。

Employee❷: ...this just _____ ____ so fast...

員工❷：...只是這一切發生的太快了...。

Manager: ...it's a _____ __ _____ ... just _____ it...

經理：...這是罕見的機會...就接受它吧...。

196

Employee❷: ...tell me what the _____ is... other than the office room...

員工❷：...告訴我優點是什麼...除了辦公室房間...。

Manager: ...there's going to be a 40% _____ in your _____... I can't say that in public...

經理：...你的薪資會有40%的調漲...我無法在大庭廣眾下說...。

Employee❷: ...seriously...? ...wow...then I will take it... I'm _____...

員工❷：...真的嗎...？...哇！...那麼我會接受它...我感到興奮...。

Manager: ...and you will have your own _____ space...

經理：...而且你會有你自己的停車空位...。

Employee❷: ..._____... now I'm feeling it... I eat my _____ up to the _____ __ I'm in... I need more wine

員工❷：...太棒了...現在我感受到了...我靠吃爬升到我現在的位置上...我需要更多的酒...。

Manager: ...you surely are...

經理：...你確實需要...。

Unit 1

工作穩定性

Instructions

❶ 請播放音檔聽下列對話，並完成試題。 MP3 047

1. What does the term, "reality check" imply?

(A) checking the difference between the real world and the virtual world.

(B) an occasion causing someone to recognize the truth in reality by correcting his misconception

(C) a situation in which a person has to be realistic.

(D) a condition in which a person's perception of reality is far from the fact.

2. What is the main topic of the conversation?

(A) the best place to listen to music

(B) the woman's lack of long-term commitment to a job

(C) young people's lack of commitment to their jobs

(D) how taking a vacation enhances working performance

3. Which of the following best describes "a job hop"?

(A) changing from one job to another frequently

(B) moving quickly in the office

(C) catching someone on the hop

(D) hopping during workout

🎋 中譯與聽力原文

Question 1-3 refer to the following conversation

Cindy:	A reality check? What do you mean?	辛蒂：	現實檢視？你是指什麼？
Jimmy:	It's time to face the music. You can't commit to a job for at least three to five years.	吉米：	是該面對現實的時候了。你對一份工作無法有3-5年的承諾。
Linda:	That's the problem, my dear. You can't make a job hop every half a year. You seem pretty unstable.	琳達：	這就是個問題，親愛的。你不能每半年就換工作。你似乎相當不穩定。
Cindy:	From HR's perspective or from your opinion. It's just not the job I think I will be doing for the next five to ten years.	辛蒂：	從人事專員的角度還是從你的意見來看。就…這不是我未來五到十年想要繼續做的工作。
Jimmy:	Perhaps you should take a vacation, figuring out what really motivates you or what you really want to do.	吉米：	或許你應該要休假，了解什麼真的能激勵你或你真的想要從事什麼？

選項中譯與解析

1. 「現實檢視」這個詞含意為何？
   (A) 檢視現實世界和虛擬世界的區別。
   (B) 透過糾正錯誤觀念，使人們認識到事實真相
   (C) 個人必須維持實際的情況。
   (D) 個人對現實的看法與事實相差甚遠。

2. 本篇談話的主旨是什麼？
   (A) 聽音樂的最佳場所。
   (B) 這位女性缺乏對工作的長期承諾。
   (C) 年輕人缺乏對工作的承諾。
   (D) 度假如何提高工作表現。

3. 以下哪個選項最能描述"job hop"?
   (A) 頻繁地換工作。
   (B) 在辦公室動作快。
   (C) 使某人措手不及。
   (D) 健身時單腳跳。

1.

· **聽到對話，直接鎖定關鍵字reality check來定位題目問題點。**此題屬於細節題及推測題，測試考生是否理解對話內容，運用換句話說，並透過對話細節推測答案，同時以刪去法解題。根據對話，figuring out what really motivates you or what you really want to do. ，可知此處的**reality指的是現實生活，特別針對工作目標**；可以先刪除錯誤的A、D選項。而此處的check，則有檢視、反省的意味，和B選項

recognize the truth：「認清現實」、correcting his misconception：「導正錯誤」等敘述相符，故此題**答案為B**。

2.

· **聽到對話，直接鎖定關鍵字job hop來定位題目問題點。**此題屬於情境題，測試考生是否理解對話內容的主題，可以利用選項的刪去法來解題。根據對話，從reality check開始話題，內容圍繞commit to a job、make a job hop；可以先刪除錯誤的A、D選項。對比B、C選項，兩者皆敘述無法投入工作，C選項針對年輕人；而B選項強調「長期」的工作，更符合對話敘述，**故答案為B**。

3.

· **聽到對話，馬上鎖定關鍵字job hop來定位問題點。**Hop，動詞「跳」，由字面的意思可以翻譯作「跳槽」。根據對話，You can't make a job hop every half a year. You seem pretty unstable.來推測，**此處的job hop指的是頻繁的換工作。**此題屬於細節題及推測題，測試考生是否理解對話內容，運用換句話說，並透過對話細節推測答案，選出意思最接近a job hop的選項。直接鎖定關鍵字job hop，根據對話，You can't make a job hop for every half a year. You seem pretty unstable.，對照A選項changing from one job to another frequently：頻繁地換工作，敘述最為相近，**故答案為A**。

Unit **2**

博物館暑期工讀申請

Instructions

❶ 請播放音檔聽下列對話，並完成試題。 MP3 048

4. Why does Jim tell the others to prepare the other documents?

(A) It is always better to be fully prepared.

(B) The more documents, the better.

(C) He wants to show off that he knows more than they do.

(D) The museum might ask for an interview after receiving the applications.

5. Why does Jim know how to apply for the position?

(A) He is a supervisor in the museum.

(B) He designed the application process.

(C) He was an intern in the museum last year.

(D) He is the curator of the museum.

6. Which of the following is NOT mentioned as one of the application materials?

(A) recommendations

(B) proof of community service

(C) GPAs

(D) online application forms

中譯與聽力原文

Questions 4-6 refer to the following conversation

Cindy: I really want to apply for a summer internship at Best Marine Museum, and I just don't know how. Should I just fill out on-line application forms?

辛蒂：我真的想要申請倍斯特海洋博物館的暑期實習，我不知道從哪開始。我只要填線上申請表格就好嗎？

Jim: That's right. But I do think you should prepare other things?

吉姆：是的。但是我認為你也該準備其他東西。

Mary: like what?

瑪莉：像是什麼？

Jim: For instance, recommendations, GPAs, and your senior project, in case there is a scheduled interview right after you apply.

吉姆：例如，推薦函、成績平均和你的大四專題，以防在你申請後有個面試安排。

Cindy: Should we prepare our passports, too?

辛蒂：我們也應該要準備護照嗎？

Jim: You should. In case you are assigned to an overseas museum.

吉姆：你應該要。以防你被分配到海外博物館。

Mary: How do you know all these?

Jim: I did it last year, and it's amazing.

瑪莉：你怎麼知道這些的？

吉姆：我去年申請的，這體驗很棒。

選項中譯與解析

4. 吉姆為何告訴其他人要準備其他文件？

(A) 準備充分總是比較好的。

(B) 文件越多越好。

(C) 他想炫耀他比他們知道得更多。

(D) 博物館收到申請後可能會要求面試。

5. 為何吉姆知道如何申請此職位？

(A) 他是博物館的主管。

(B) 他設計申請步驟。

(C) 去年他在博物館實習。

(D) 他是博物館館長。

6. 關於申請材料，下列選項中何者未被提及？

(A) 推薦函。

(B) 社區服務證明。

(C) 平均成績。

(D) 線上申請表格。

4.

・聽到對話，直接鎖定**in case there is a scheduled interview, right after you apply.** 可知其他文件的事先準備，是為了以防萬一，申請後會馬上有面試要準備，**故此題答案為D**。此題屬於細節題，題目詢問準備資料的目的，可以直接鎖定連詞in case：「萬一」，找到關鍵字interview。根據對話in case there is a scheduled interview, right after you apply.，最符合選項D的敘述：「博物館在收到申請後可能會要求面試」。故此題**答案為D**。

5.

・聽到對話，馬上鎖定**I did it last year**。根據對話問答：How do you know all these?；I did it last year, and it's amazing.可知Jim去年申請過並通過了博物館實習，所以**此題答案為C**。此題屬於細節題，測試考生是否理解對話內容，並判斷說話者的身分。根據對話，由apply for a summer internship開始話題，可知對話關鍵在internship：「實習」，所以此處的I did it last year表示他去年曾去實習過了，和C選項的敘述相符，故答案為C。(A) supervisor：監督人；(C) intern：實習生；(D) curator：館長。

6.

・聽到對話，馬上鎖定關鍵字**application materials**：申請資料。根據對話，application forms、 recommendations、 GPAs、senior project和passport可知此題**答案為B**。此題屬於細節題，考生須由題目一一對照對話，判斷選項是否正確。此題關鍵在application materials，題目詢問對話「未」提及的申請資料。根據對話內容，答案為B選項社區服務證明。(A) recommendations，推薦函；(C) GPAs，平均成績；(D) online application forms線上申請表。

Unit 3
神經大條，
得罪大咖也不曉得

Instructions

❶ 請播放音檔聽下列對話，並完成試題。 🎧 MP3 049

7. What is the woman's problem?
    (A) She sat at the wrong table.
    (B) She offended an important business partner.
    (C) She ordered the wrong meal.
    (D) She was rude to her co-worker.

8. Where might this conversation take place?
    (A) in a restaurant
    (B) in an airport
    (C) in an airline company
    (D) in a bank

9. Why is Best Airline the only airline their company is doing business with?
    (A) Another airline the company used to do business with went bankrupt and their partnership was terminated.
    (B) Best Airline gave the company the best deal.
    (C) Best Airline specializes in transporting lightweight products.
    (D) The company stopped doing business with another airline because of security breaches.

🍀 中譯與聽力原文

Questions 7-9 refer to the following conversation

Judy: You shouldn't be rude to him.

茱蒂：你不該對他這麼無禮。

Mary: Why?

瑪莉：為什麼？

Judy: He owns Best Airline. That's why. You're aware that most of our products are lightweight, and 90% of our products are heavily reliant on airplane to export.

茱蒂：他擁有倍斯特航空公司。這就是理由。你有察覺到大部分我們的產品都輕，且我們百分之九十的產品都仰賴飛機出口。

Mary: Oh... Crap... I have no idea. But he obviously has no idea who I am. I think we'll be fine. Relax.

瑪莉：喔...糟了...我不知道。但是他顯然不知道我是誰。我想我們會沒事。放輕鬆。

Jim: Based on the table we're sitting at and whom we are sitting with, I think he knows.

吉姆：根據我們坐的餐桌位子和我們跟誰坐，我想他知道。

Mary: Please tell me that Best Airline is not the only airline we've been having businesses with.

瑪莉：請告訴我倍斯特航空公司不是我們唯一有商業往來的航空公司。

Judy: After ABG Airline announced bankruptcy the other day, it's the only one.

茱蒂：在前幾天ABG航空公司宣告破產的後，這就是我們唯一合作的公司。

選項中譯與解析

7. 女子出了什麼問題？

    (A) 她坐錯位置。

    (B) 她冒犯了重要的商業夥伴。

    (C) 她點錯了餐。

    (D) 她對同事無禮。

8. 本篇對話可能發生的地點？

    (A) 在餐廳。

    (B) 在機場。

    (C) 在航空公司。

    (D) 在銀行。

9. 為何倍斯特航空公司是他們公司唯一合作的航空公司？

    (A) 曾和公司有業務往來的航空公司破產，因此合作關係終止。

    (B) 倍斯特航空公司給這間公司的條件最好。

    (C) 倍斯特航空公司專門運輸輕量產品。

    (D) 因為安全漏洞，公司終止和另一家航空公司的生意。

7.

・聽到對話，馬上鎖定**You shouldn't be rude to him.**和**He owns Best Airline.**推測她可能得罪了**Best Airline**的老闆。以關鍵字be rude to和having businesses with配對選項的**offended**：得罪以及

business partner，**可知此題答案為B**。此題為細節題，考生須先理解 be rude to Sb的意思，表示對誰無禮；接著推測對話發生的情境。可以先排除較明顯錯誤的A、C選項，接著判斷人物關係。根據對話細節，be rude to him接著延伸He owns Best Airline、we've been having businesses with推測她可能得罪了公司的合作對象。

8.

· **聽到對話，直接鎖定the table we're sitting at and whom we are sitting with，來推測對話發生的情境。**根據關鍵字the table：餐桌，配對選項a restaurant，可以推測**最符合答案的選項即為A**。此題為推測題，測試考生是否能透過對話細節，推測出對話發生的地點。根據對話：Based on the table we're sitting at and whom we are sitting with來配對選項，從關鍵字the table來判斷，最適合的答案即為選項 (A)restaurant：餐廳。

9.

· **聽到對話，直接鎖定關鍵字bankruptcy**：名詞，破產。根據對話，After ABG Airline announced bankruptcy the other day, it's the only one.可知在ABG航空公司宣告破產後，Best Airline是他們唯一合作的公司。此題為細節題，考生須先理解動詞片語announced bankruptcy的用法，接著找出他的相似詞來推測答案，也可以搭配刪去法解答。根據關鍵字**announced bankruptcy：宣告破產**，配對選項A的went bankrupt：破產，和their partnership was terminated；terminated在這句是過去分詞，和be動詞was搭配形成被動語態，表達「被終止」，**可知答案即為A**。(B) gave the best deal：給最好的折扣；(C)specializes in：專攻；(D)security breaches：安全漏洞。

Unit 4

角逐西岸職缺

Instructions

❶ 請播放音檔聽下列對話，並完成試題。 🎧 MP3 050

10. **What does the man mean when he says, "I was wondering if you could put in a few good words for me"?**

(A) He wanted to know if the other man can give him some compliments.

(B) He wanted to know if the other man can show him how to give compliments.

(C) He wanted to know if the other man can say something nice about him to help with his application

(D) He wanted to know if the other man can teach him how to use good words in his application documents.

11. **What does the man mean by saying, "But I don't have a say in this"?**

(A) He does not want to give the other man the application information

(B) He does not know how to explain the application process

(C) He does not have the power to decide who gets the new position

(D) He does not want to say good words about the other man

12. **Which of the following is the closest in meaning to "Lots of people are eyeing that job"?**

(A) Lots of people have good eyesight in this company.

(B) Lots of people are aiming to get that new position

(C) Many co-workers dislike their current jobs.

(D) Many co-workers are thinking about moving to the west coast.

🍃 中譯與聽力原文

Questions 10-12 refer to the following conversation

Mark:	I didn't mean to eavesdrop, but I heard we're having a new position at our branch office.	馬克：	我不是有意偷聽，但是我聽到分公司有個新的職缺。
Jim:	Yep... the West Coast... you sound intrigued.	吉姆：	是的…西岸…你看起來像對這很有興趣。
Mark:	You got me. I'm thinking about moving to the West Coast. I was wondering if you could put in a few good words for me.	馬克：	被你發現了。我正考慮要搬至西岸。我思考著你能否替我美言幾句。
Jim:	But I don't have a say in this. Why don't you ask Jane? She is our HR manager. She's been	吉姆：	但是關於這件事我沒有決定權。為什麼你不問簡呢？她是人事部門經

211

here since the company launched.

理。從公司創立待到現在。

Mark: She doesn't seem like my big fan.

馬克：她似乎不太喜歡我。

Jim: But if you want to do that job, you'd better talk to her right now. Lots of people are eyeing that job.

吉姆：但是如果你想要這份工作的話，你最好現在跟她說。許多人都覬覦那份工作。

選項中譯與解析

10. 當男子說「我思考著是否你能替我美言幾句。」，其含意為何？

(A) 他想知道對方人是否讚美他幾句。

(B) 他想知道對方是否能教他如何讚美。

(C) 他想知道對方是否能美言幾句，以利於他的申請。

(D) 他想知道對方是否能教他如何在申請文件中用詞精煉。

11. 對話中的男子說「但是關於這件事我沒有決定權」，其含意為何？

(A) 他不想提供申請資訊給對方。

(B) 他不知道如何解釋申請步驟。

(C) 他無權決定誰能獲得新職位。

(D) 他不想替其方説好話。

12. 下列選項中，何者最接近「許多人都覬覦那份工作」？

(A) 公司裡很多人視力良好。

(B) 很多人對新職缺躍躍欲試。

(C) 許多同事不喜歡目前的工作。

(D) 許多同事正考慮搬到西岸。

10.

· **聽到對話，馬上鎖定put in a few good words for me**，推測是「替我說好話」的意思。此題屬於推測題，測試考生對慣用語 **"put in a few good words"** 的理解，考生必須先懂這個慣用語的深層意思，再推測哪個選項描述的意思最接近此慣用語。考點引用句的另一線索字是for me，所以put in a few good words for me是他希望另一位男士替他說好話，(C)選項完整句句意和此引用句最接近。**選項(A)及(B)的compliments是陷阱字**，雖然是「讚美」之意，似乎與good words意思類似，但這兩句的完整句句意都不符合考點的引用句， (A) ... give him some compliments是「（直接）給他讚美」，(B) ... show him how to give compliments，「示範給他看如何給（別人）讚美」。(D)也有句意不合的錯誤，而且引用句沒有牽涉到application documents。

11.

· **聽到對話，馬上鎖定 don't have a say**，由於say前面搭配動詞have及冠詞a，由此得知say在此轉換成名詞，意思和say當動詞時「說」的意思不同。此題屬於推測題，主要從慣用語have a say，「有決定權」推測。而且正確選項必須呼應主題。此對話主題是討論如何爭取新職位。(A)和(B)的application information/process是陷阱字，雖然申請職位或許需要獲得申請資訊，但整段對話完全沒有關於申請資訊或過程的描述。(D)選項敘述大意是「他不想替另一位男士說好話」與have a say意思無關。**唯一最貼切主題的選項是(C)**。

12.

· **考慮主題是爭取新職位，只有(B)選項描述最貼近主題，故正確選項是(B)**。此題屬於推測題，主要從慣用語eye ...，「著眼於......，將目標放在......」推測。與此片語意思最接近的是(B)的動詞片語aim to V.。(A)選項的eyesight視力，是陷阱字，雖然此複合字有eye，但和eye for的意思及詞性不同。且(A)及(C)敘述完全無關對話主題。(D)的west coast也是陷阱字，根據對話，新職位在西岸，但(D)大意是「許多同事正考慮搬到西岸」，若選擇(D)就犯下過度詮釋的錯誤。而且根據I'm thinking about moving to the West Coast，我們能確定的是只有講者一人正考慮搬到西岸。

Unit 5
換個角度想，
有得必有失

Instructions

❶ 請播放音檔聽下列對話，並完成試題。 MP3 051

13. Which of the following is the main factor that decides whether the man gets the job?

(A) talking to Jane

(B) filing for a new evaluation process

(C) moving to the west coast first

(D) the evaluation of his performance

14. Who are these speakers?

(A) HR agents

(B) co-workers

(C) accountants

(D) travel agents

15. Which of the following is the closest in meaning to "lucrative"?

(A) very valuable

(B) priceless

(C) worthwhile

(D) very profitable

🍂 中譯與聽力原文

Questions 13-15 refer to the following conversation

Mark: I think you're right about one thing... lots of people are eye-ing that job. How can I get that job? I talked to Jane, apparently, she told me it will go accord-ing to the evaluation sheets and company procedures.

馬克： 我認為你說對一件事了…許多人都覬覦那個工作。要怎樣才能拿到這份工作呢？我詢問過簡，她說一切都會照著評估表和公司流程走。

Jim: there is nothing I can do. But look on the bright side. You don't have to take a huge pay cut. The reason why other people are applying is because of the pay increase.

吉姆： 我也無能為力。但是往好處想。你不用擔心大幅的減薪。其他人會想申請的原因是因為薪資增加。

Mark: yep it seems lucrative to them. Perhaps I should rethink about moving to the West Coast.

馬克： 是的似乎對他們來說很有利可圖的。或許我應該要重新思考搬到西岸的事。

Jim: let's just watch the game and have some chicken wings.

吉姆： 讓我們就只看場球賽然後來些雞翅吧。

選項中譯與解析

13. 關於決定男子是否能得到這份工作，下列選項何者是主因？

    (A) 和珍談談。

    (B) 申請新的評估步驟。

    (C) 先移居到西岸。

    (D) 針對表現評估。

14. 這些談話者是誰？

    (A) 人資代表。

    (B) 同事。

    (C) 會計師。

    (D) 旅行社員工。

15. 下列選項中，何者最接近**"lucrative"**？

    (A) 非常有價值的。

    (B) 無價的。

    (C) 值得做的。

    (D) 非常有利可圖的。

13.

‧ 聽到對話，馬上鎖定**it will go according to the evaluation sheets and company procedures**，推測是「跟公司規定有關」的意思。此題屬於文意理解題，針對兩人對話中的內容，而選出接近的答案，難度不高。考點引用句的另一線索字是evaluation sheets，評估表和company procedures，工作流程，照著評估表和流程來是否能得到工作。因此，可以推斷出工作表現很重要。而選項(A)talking to

Jane，是用來混淆，因為此句話重點是簡後面說的話，並非代表和她講完後，就能得到工作。選項(C)moving to the west coast first 則是馬克之後要考慮之事。

14.

· 聽到對話，馬上鎖定**job**，**evaluation sheets and company procedures**，**a huge pay cut**，推測和「工作方面」有關。此題屬於推測題，也同時測試考生對於對話理解程度，此題囊括所有內容，很容易被誤導。考點分析。對話中兩人提到幾個線索。(1) eyeing that job...，覬覦那個工作 (2) I talked to Jane...，我詢問過簡 (3) go according to the evaluation sheets and company procedures...，照著評估表 和公司流程走 (4) the reason why other people are applying is because of the pay increase...，其他人會想申請的原因是因為薪資增加， 因此推測出來兩人是同事關係。選項(A) HR agents，是陷阱選項。

15.

· 聽到對話，馬上鎖定**because of the pay increase**，因為薪資增加，推測是「利益」的意思。此題屬於單字理解題，也同時測試考生對單字理解，通常單字意思接近，造成考生混淆，再推測哪個選項描述的意思最接近考題。"lucrative" 的意思為「有利可圖的」，假設不知道這單字的意思，仍然可以從四個選項中判斷出答案。通常此種單字考法，其中兩到三個選項的意思會類似，如：valuable和worthwhile， 因此可採刪去法，再來一一突破。

Unit 6

事情辦得好，
升遷就有份

Instructions

❶ 請播放音檔聽下列對話，並完成試題。 🎧 MP3 052

16. Who might this woman be?

    (A) the man's wife

    (B) the man's supervisor

    (C) the man's assistant

    (D) the man's girlfriend

17. Why does the man say, "I'm considering giving you a promotion"?

    (A) He just thinks it's about time that the woman is promoted.

    (B) He is very satisfied with the woman's performance.

    (C) The woman has been asking for a promotion for several months.

    (D) Everyone is promoted except the woman.

18. Where will the man take a transfer?

    (A) Hong Kong

    (B) Dubai

    (C) Los Angeles

    (D) Singapore

中譯與聽力原文

Questions 16-18 refer to the following conversation

Mary: I'm here to give you some update. I've booked your flight to Dubai. You're going to take a transfer at HK. I wrote a note to our sales manager that the weekly meeting will be postponed. I'm gonna get the dry cleaning for you.

瑪莉： 我是要跟您報告最新狀況。我已經訂購您到杜拜的班機。您會於香港轉機。我寫了字條給我們的銷售經理，每週會議會延期。我會替您取送洗衣物。

Jason: It seems that you handle things pretty well lately.

傑森： 看來您最近處理事情都處理得相當妥善。

Mary: it's nothing, doing the usual routine, and I forgot to tell you about the financial reports. The Accounting managers won't be able to give us those reports until next Monday.

瑪莉： 這沒什麼，只是平常的例行事務，我忘了要跟您說財政報告的事。會計經理們要到下星期一才能將那些報告給我們。

Jason: You know what... if things keep going like this I'm considering giving you a promotion.

傑森： 你知道嗎？...如果事情都像這樣的話，我正考慮升遷妳。

16. 女子可能的身分為何？

　　(A) 男子的老婆。

　　(B) 男子的主管。

　　(C) 男子的助理。

　　(D) 男子的女友。

17. 為何男子說「我正考慮升遷妳」？

　　(A) 他只是認為該是女子升遷的時候了。

　　(B) 他對女子的表現非常滿意。

　　(C) 女子一直要求升遷幾個月了。

　　(D) 除了女子外，每個人都已被升遷了。

18. 男子將在在哪裡轉機？

　　(A) 香港。

　　(B) 杜拜。

　　(C) 洛杉磯。

　　(D) 新加坡。

16.

・聽到 **who**，馬上鎖定詢問關係，推測是此女子身分為何。此題屬於推測題，由前面第一句瑪莉說的話：我是要跟您報告最新狀況和最後一句傑森說：我正考慮升遷妳，可推知答案。考點是 supervisor，主管和 assistant，助理。女子跟男子報告例行事物，如：I'm here to give you some update. 和 tell you about the financial...，財政報告的事，這些都提供非常有用的線索，**可推測女子是助理**。男子說：I'm considering giving you a promotion，我正考慮升遷妳，顯然他是上司或主管。

17.

· **聽到對話，馬上鎖定，promotion 推測是「工作」方面。**此題屬於推測題，首先必須先懂得"considering giving you a promotion"的理解，考生必須先懂此句話的深層意思，再推測哪個選項描述的意思最接近此含意。be satisfied with Sb.，對某人感到滿意。上司對話中提到：It seems that you handle things pretty well lately.，看來妳最近處理事情都處理得相當妥善。以及：if things keep going like this，如果事情都像這樣的話，後面提到升遷。因此推知，對於此女子的工作表現認可，**故答案為選項為(B)**。

18.

· **聽到單字transfer 馬上鎖定飛機或地點，注意聽之後的單字。**這題是屬於「單字題」聽的時候，可以馬上得知答案。此題屬於地點考法，也同時測試考生對單字認識多寡。第一重點是transfer，轉機，第二重點是地點Hong Kong，香港。考點引用句的另一線索字是HK，HK是香港縮寫，因此選項中並未用HK，而是寫Hong Kong。聽力一個小技巧，先瀏覽過答案，可以加深對聽力的理解力。本題是很好的範例，如果先看地點，聽對話時，則對transfer 特別注意。

1 新多益基礎對話演練

2 新多益單篇對話和解析

3 新多益對話模擬試題

Unit 7

醜陋牆還不如美麗牆

 Instructions

❶ 請播放音檔聽下列對話，並完成試題。 ▶ MP3 053

19. What does "an ugly wall" refer to in this context?

   (A) a wall that is not painted well and ugly

   (B) a wall that displays pictures of natural sceneries

   (C) a wall that looks very shabby

   (D) a wall that displays photos in which people don't look their best

20. Why does the man say, "It's so inappropriate"?

   (A) He feels angry that he was humiliated.

   (B) He doesn't think it's nice to feel good by mocking others.

   (C) An ugly wall is not a proper name for this activity.

   (D) A beauty wall is inappropriate.

21. What might the speakers do next?

   (A) take away the photos on the ugly wall

   (B) learn how to use photo editing APPs

   (C) gather employees' photos in which they look good

   (D) paint the ugly wall so that it will look better

中譯與聽力原文

Questions 19-21 refer to the following conversation

Jason: I can't believe they're having an ugly wall.

傑森：我不敢相信我們有醜陋牆。

Mary: What's that? A wall that's ugly.

瑪莉：那是什麼？很醜的牆？

Jason: Putting a bunch of pictures, making fun of someone.

傑森：放些照片，取笑其他人為樂。

Jim: How did they get all of the employees' photos?

吉姆：他們怎麼有所有員工的照片呢？

Mary: Probably from annual meetings and casual Friday dinners.

瑪莉：可能是從年度會議和隨興的星期五晚餐。

Jim: It's so inappropriate. Humiliating someone in exchange for pleasure.

吉姆：這很不恰當。羞辱別人以換取樂趣。

Jason: Perhaps we can do a beauty wall, using photo editing devices.

傑森：或許我們可以弄個美貌牆，使用照片編輯裝置。

Mary: Why not everyone looks great, and it won't be hidden in some

瑪莉：為什麼不能？每個人看起來很棒，而且不會藏

| place we can't quite figure out. | 在我們無法找到的某些地方。 |

| Jason: | That rocks! | 傑森：棒呆了。 |

 選項中譯與解析

19. 根據對話，**"an ugly wall"** 是指什麼？

(A) 沒刷好又醜的牆

(B) 展示自然風景面的牆壁

(C) 看起來很破舊的牆

(D) 展出人們狀態不佳照的一道牆

20. 為何男子說「這很不恰當」？

(A) 他因被羞辱感到生氣。

(B) 他不認為羞辱別人感覺會有多好。

(C) 醜陋牆不適合這個活動名稱。

(D) 美貌牆不合適。

21. 談話者接下來可能會做何事？

(A) 把醜陋牆上的照片拿走

(B) 學習如何使用照片編輯裝置

(C) 收集員工看起來美美的照片

(D) 粉刷醜陋牆，如此看起來好多了

19.

・聽到對話，馬上鎖定 **ugly wall** 和 **what's that** 推測是真正意思。此題屬於推測題，此種推測題，通常在對話中會出現一問一答。考生掌握對話的問題，仔細聽回答，再推測哪個選項描述的意思最接近此答案。考

點引用句的另一線索字是photo，四個選項中，只有**選項(D)**...displays photos... 出現。另外一個重點，ugly wall直接翻譯是醜牆，通常答案不會是直翻，會有陷阱。因此，聽到女子問What's that? 男子回答Putting a bunch of pictures, making fun of someone. 可推測出來。

20.

· **聽到對話，馬上鎖定inappropriate和其後面的對話 Humiliating someone in exchange of...，推測是「不滿，不適合」的意思。** 此題屬於推測題，也同時測試考生對單字"humiliate"和"mock"的理解。考生必須先懂這個單字的意思，再推測哪個選項描述的意思最接近此意。考點引用句的另一線索字是Humiliating someone，羞辱別人，看到(A)... that he was humiliated..., (D) A beauty wall...，刪去(A)&(D)，因為談話者並沒有被羞辱，以及beauty wall和主題不和。再比較(B) & (C)，刪去(C)，因為(C)a proper name... 意思是針對活動名稱，所以**(B)**He doesn't think it's nice...「他不認為...好」是最佳選項。

21.

· **聽到對話，馬上鎖定 對話最後的幾句，推測是進行「美貌牆」之事。** 此題屬於推測題，也同時測試考生對前後語意關聯的理解，考生必須了解幾句話的關聯性，再選出最接近的選項。考點引用句的另一線索字是do a beauty wall，所以有可能的答案，和此有關。本題有點弔詭，四個選項都和對話有連結。因此，必須用刪去法，選出最適合並最合理的答案。(A) take away the photos on the ugly wall → 這不是接下來要做。(B) learn how to use photo editing APPs→ 文中提到使用，表示已會使用。(C) gather employees' photos in which they look good→ 因為美貌牆，必須用美照。(D) paint the ugly wall so that it will look better→ 這跟牆壁本身無關。

Unit 8

銷售打賭，
鹿死誰手還不曉得

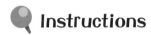

Instructions

❶ 請播放音檔聽下列對話，並完成試題。 MP3 054

22. What is the main topic of the conversation?

    (A) paying back mortgage and tuition

    (B) booking a hotel

    (C) making money in an exhibition

    (D) printing pamphlets

23. What does the man mean by saying, "I'll have more incentives to do things"?

    (A) He will feel more motivated.

    (B) He feels the company should give him more incentives.

    (C) The exhibition should offer more incentives to workers.

    (D) He will have more bonuses.

24. Which of the following is the place where they will make their earnings?

    (A) a printing plant

    (B) a booking center

    (C) a construction site

    (D) a computer exhibition

🌿 中譯與聽力原文

Questions 22-24 refer to the following conversation

Jack: You are aware that we are working on a commission. The more we sell at a computer exhibition, the more we earn. The exhibition only opens for fourteen days. Why don't you grab this chance and earn as much as you can in half a month?

傑克：你有察覺到我們工作是抽成嗎？在電腦展，我們販售的越多，就賺越多。這個展覽僅開幕14天而已。為什麼你不抓住這機會，在半個月內盡可能地賺？

Mark: I get it. Sometimes it's hard to think that way. Perhaps I should think more about the mortgage and tuition fees, then I'll have more incentives to do things.

馬克：我懂了。有時候真的很難這樣思考。或許我應該要思考更多關於抵押貸款和學費，然後有更多的動機去做事。

Mary: that's a good start.

瑪莉：這是個好的開始。

Jack: Let's have a bet. Who sells the most computers in fourteen days wins, and who sells the least gets punished.

傑克：讓我們來打賭。誰在14天裡賣最多的獲勝，而誰賣得最少的受到懲罰。

| Mary: | I've got to warn you that I've already sold more than you two combined. | 瑪莉：我必須提醒你們我已經賣出比你們兩個人加起來還多台了。 |

選項中譯與解析

22. 對話的主題為何？

(A) 償還抵押貸款和學費。

(B) 飯店預約。

(C) 在展覽中賺錢。

(D) 印刷小冊子。

23. 男子說「我會有更多的動機去做事」，其含意為何？

(A) 他會感覺更有動力。

(B) 他覺得公司應該給他更多的獎勵。

(C) 展覽應該提供員工更多獎勵。

(D) 他將獲得更多獎金。

24. 下列選項中，何者是他們賺錢之處？

(A) 印刷廠。

(B) 訂票中心。

(C) 建築工地。

(D) 電腦展。

22.

· 聽到對話，馬上鎖定 **main topic** 兩字，為「主旨」的意思。此題屬於主旨考法，是針對對話所有內容，因此將聽到的重要單字，進行連結，才能理解題意。如：computer exhibition，電腦展，The more we sell at..., the more we earn.，我們販售的越多，就賺越多，也同時測試考生對於對話的理解。此種考法的好處為，即使單字並不全部理解，卻能從對話中，推測出談論之事。考點引用句的另一線索字是 grab this chance and earn as much as you can ...，所以earn這個單字非常重要。希望賺錢之意。(A)選項對話中有提到，不過是陷阱。選項(B)及(D)則和主題無關，針對 computer exhibition電腦展，earn和sell幾個字，推測之來他們討論在展覽中賺錢，**答案為選項(C)**。

23.

‧**聽到對話，馬上鎖定mortgage and tuition fees，推測和「還貸款及學費」有關聯。**此題屬於單字推測題，也同時測試考生對單字的理解。透過考單字，讓考生推出選項中意思接近的答案。考點引用句的另一線索字是incentive，動力的，對話中女子提到貸款和學費，這兩點讓她有動機去電腦展銷售。**選項(A)更有動力。**選項(B)...incentive和題目單字一樣，然而意思不同。選項(C)incentive，在此是指獎勵。選項(D)bonus，在此指獎金或獎勵。因此，選項(B)(C)(D)皆出現陷阱字，請小心。

24.

‧**本題重點是 place，推測「地點」之意。**此題屬於推測題，也同時測試考生對於對話的地點理解。此類型題目，對於整篇對話掌握度必須很強，因此通常答案不會「直接」出現在對話裡。考點引用句的重要線索句是The more we sell at a computer exhibition, the more we earn.，在電腦展，我們販售的越多，就賺越多。因此，推測出他們將在電腦展販售商品。 此類型考題有兩種考法，第一種，破題型：對話中直接講出地點。第二種：透過對話描述和暗示，讓考生推測出地點。本題是第一種考法，比較簡單，分數應該要掌握。

Unit 9

烤雞事業，東京也設點

Instructions

❶ 請播放音檔聽下列對話，並完成試題。 🎧 MP3 055

25. Where does the conversation take place?

    (A) a chicken farm

    (B) Tokyo

    (C) a restaurant

    (D) a coffee shop

26. Who is the woman?

    (A) a chef

    (B) a customer

    (C) a writer

    (D) an editor

27. What does the man mean by saying, "It's been ages"?

    (A) It has been a long time.

    (B) He is aging quickly.

    (C) The recipe for the roast chicken is very old.

    (D) Aging is unavoidable.

中譯與聽力原文

Questions 25-27 refer to the following conversation

Jim: It's been ages. What brings you down here?

吉姆：已經好久不見。是什麼風把你吹來這裡？

Mary: I haven't tasted your roast chicken for quite a bit, and the wine. It really is a perfect blend. Just out of curiosity, how do you do so well in both family and business?

瑪莉：我有相當久沒有嚐到這裡的烤雞，還有酒了。這搭配真是完美的組合。出於好奇，你怎麼能在家庭跟事業上都做得這麼好？

Jim: It would be a lie, if I answered it's probably nothing. It takes efforts. By the way, would you like to come to our new opening in Tokyo. By then, we will be having another two special dishes. I suppose for a big fan of roast chicken like you, you certainly can't say "NO".

吉姆：如果我回答這可能沒什麼，那我就是在說謊。這是需要努力的。附帶一提的是，你會想要來我們東京的開幕嗎？到那時候我們會有另外兩個特別餐點。我想像你這樣的烤雞迷，你確實無法說「不」。

Mary: Terrific. I'd love to.

瑪莉：棒極了。我會想去。

選項中譯與解析

25. 本篇對話發生的地點？

    (A) 養雞場。

    (B) 東京。

    (C) 餐廳。

    (D) 咖啡店。

26. 女子職業為何？

    (A) 廚師。

    (B) 顧客。

    (C) 作家。

    (D) 編輯。

27. 男子說「已經好久了」，含意為何？

    (A) 時間過了很久。

    (B) 他老的很快。

    (C) 烤雞食譜很古老。

    (D) 老化是無法避免的。

25.

· 聽到對話，馬上鎖定 **take place**，是「發生」的意思，推測考地點。此題屬於推測題，(A) a chicken farm，養雞場，(B) Tokyo，東京，(C) a restaurant餐廳，(D) a coffee shop咖啡廳，我們先將(A)和(B)刪除，因此對話是討論roast chicken 和new opening，新開幕，故推知是他們在餐廳類的場所。考點引用句的另一線索字是our new opening，這裡的new opening 是指「新開幕」，不是打開之一。選項(A) a chicken farm養雞場，只是誤導，因為對話中提到roast chicken。選項(B) Tokyo，東京，對話中提到new opening in Tokyo 是指在東京的開幕，因此不可能是此時談話之處。選項(D) a coffee shop咖啡廳，也是類似的地點，不過對話中提到烤雞，因此餐廳較適合。

26.

· 聽到對話，馬上鎖定**who**，推測是問「**職業或關係**」的意思。選項(C) a writer，作家和選項(D)an editor，編輯，和對話無關，可以先刪除。(A) a chef 和(B) a customer兩者有關聯。由女子説：I haven't tasted your roast chicken，我已經很久沒有品嚐這裡的烤雞了...，得知**答案為(B)**。此題屬於關聯題，考學生對於談話中的男女，兩者間有何關係。因此，先刪掉不相關的選項，再進行選擇。考點引用句的另一線索是 taste，品嚐和roast chicken，烤雞，對話中，女子説「已經很久沒嚐這裡的烤雞了，還有酒。」，以及詢問對方：how can you do so well in both family and business...「你怎麼能在家庭跟事業上都做得這麼好」，推知她是顧客，而男子是老闆，或是廚師。

27.

· 聽到對話，馬上鎖定**ages**，推測是「**年紀，時間久**」的意思。選項中，此題屬於推測題，除了選項(A)(C)，均出現和age 相關單字，如：aging。此為陷阱，讓考生再第一印象中，選出此錯誤答案。It's been ages. 是指時間已經好久了，也同時測試考生對慣用語 "It's been ages"的理解，考點引用句的另一線索字是for quite a bit，此句也有好久之意。age 意思多元，除了有年紀之意，還可指「很長時間」。選項(B)... aging quickly，是指老化得快。選項(C) The recipe... is very old..是指「食譜古老」，選項(D) Aging is unavoidable.「老化是無可避免的。」此三字皆為引導錯誤方向，請小心選擇。

Unit 10

新人誤事，狀況連連

Instructions

❶ 請播放音檔聽下列對話，並完成試題。  MP3 056

28. Where does the conversation take place?

(A) a shopping mall

(B) an airplane

(C) an airline counter

(D) a travel agency

29. What company might those speakers work for?

(A) a cafeteria

(B) an airline

(C) a travel agency

(D) a restaurant

30. Why are meal tickets and coupons mentioned?

(A) The speakers are hungry.

(B) The speakers want to buy meals with coupons.

(C) The speakers are launching a marketing campaign by giving away meal tickets and coupons.

(D) The speakers try to appease the customers with meal tickets and coupons.

中譯與聽力原文

Questions 28-30 refer to the following conversation

Linda: I just don't want to burden you with this.

琳達：我只是不想讓你感到負擔。

Tina: Excuse me? burden me? You have such a serious problem, and you don't come for help.

緹娜：不好意思？成為我的負擔？你這問題嚴重了，而你卻不求助。

Linda: You guys are so busy... since I'm so new here. I just assumed things will turn out to be ok.

琳達：你們都很忙碌...既然我是這裡新來的。我只是設想成事情最後會沒事。

Tina: All flights are overbooked. I just don't know what to do.

緹娜：所有班機都超賣。我真的不知道該怎麼做。

Mark: I've checked with other ground crews. Customers are gonna lose it.

馬克：我已經與地勤人員確認過了。顧客要失控了。

Tina: I'm considering shutting down the system.

緹娜：我已經考慮到要先關閉系統。

Mark: Have Jack on line 2, and Cindy on line 3. Perhaps it's system errors.

馬克：傑克在2線，然後辛蒂在三線。或許是系統錯誤。

| Tina: | Prepare meal tickets and coupons to calm those passengers. | 緹娜：準備餐卷和優惠卷安撫那些乘客。 |

選項中譯與解析

28. 本篇對話發生的地點？

(A) 購物中心。

(B) 飛機上。

(C) 航空公司櫃檯。

(D) 旅行社。

29. 那些談話者可能是替哪個類型的公司工作？

(A) 自助餐廳。

(B) 航空公司。

(C) 旅行社。

(D) 餐廳。

30. 為何提到餐券和優惠券？

(A) 談話者者肚子餓了。

(B) 談話者想用優惠券買餐點。

(C) 談話者正舉辦贈送餐券和優惠券的行銷活動。

(D) 談話者嘗試用餐券和優惠券安撫顧客。

28.

．聽到對話，馬上鎖定 **overbooked**和**ground crews**，推測和「飛機或機場」有關。此題屬於推測題，對話中提到，system errors，系統錯誤，all flights，所有班機，overbooked超賣，這幾個字，因此可推論出地點是和「飛機」有關。由第一點鎖定地勤，因此選項(B)飛機上答

案不符合，因此**選項(C)** an airline counter，在航空公司櫃檯最有可能。考點引用句的另一線索字是，看到(A) a shopping mall購物中心，先刪掉，因為是和航班方面有關。選項(D)a travel agency旅行社，對話中提到 Customers are gonna lose it.顧客要失控了。gonna = going to，lose 在此為lose control指「失控」。綜合以上觀點，可以將飛機上的可能刪掉。

29.

· **聽到對話，馬上鎖定 company，推測問「公司」。**承上題，兩人討論超賣，顧客失控以及對話中有句：I'm so new here，我是新來的，推知她在航空公司工作。此題屬於推測題，也同時測試考生對常用單字的理解，考生必須先懂這些單字，再加以融會貫通，才能推測哪個選項描述的意思最接近此答案。考點引用句的另一線索字是…I'm new here.，我是新來的，已知單字和機場和票務方面有關，因此選項(B)an airline，航空公司，和(C)a travel agency，旅行社，都有可能。另外一個重點為：單字ground crews地勤，因此推知**選項(B)**航空公司最佳。

30.

· **聽到對話，馬上鎖定 meal tickets and coupons，推測是這些物品的用途。**由對話最後一句提到：calm those passengers 安撫顧客，所以**(D)…to appease the customers with meal tickets and coupons.「用餐券和優惠券安撫顧客」是最佳選項。**此題屬於細節及推測題，測試考生對動詞calm的理解，及能否找出calm的類似字，再推測哪個選項描述的意思最接近。calm和appease都有「安撫」之意。考點引用句的另一線索是：system errors，系統錯誤，和 lose，失去，由於航空公司失誤導致問題，造成Customers are gonna lost it.，顧客要失控了。因此採取某些措施來安撫他們。

Unit 11
休假，
同事就是要多擔待

Instructions

❶ 請播放音檔聽下列對話，並完成試題。 🎧 MP3 057

31. Why does the man say "sorry" to the other two speakers?
   (A) because the others have to cover for him
   (B) because he is sorry that he did a lousy job
   (C) because his work is a mess
   (D) because the vacation did not go well

32. Which of the following details is NOT mentioned regarding the work duties?
   (A) wire transfer
   (B) target customers
   (C) booking a flight
   (D) sending flowers

33. Why can't the man do the work by himself?
   (A) He is going to quit his job.
   (B) He is going to take a sick leave.
   (C) He is going on a vacation.
   (D) His mental condition is not stable.

中譯與聽力原文

Questions 31-33 refer to the following conversation

Jack: I'm taking a vacation from Dec. 15 to Dec 25. Sorry that you have to do the job while I'm on a vacation.

傑克：我將於12月15日到12月25日休假。抱歉在我休假時，你們要做我的工作。

Jim: We saw the note. Best Company only accepts a wire transfer. It has to be made on Dec. 16. We're targeting our customers on a younger viewer, a drastic change from the past. Send flowers to congratulate Sales Director of ABC, two days after you take the vacation.

吉姆：我們看到註了。倍斯特公司款項僅收電匯。要在12月16日完成。我們目標顧客是年輕觀眾，與去年相對是極大的改變。你休假的兩天後，寄送花朵給ABC公司的銷售負責人。

Mary: I have two more questions. You didn't write contact information of the flower shop. This is a credit card payment from the last business trip (Dec 17) you forgot to tell the accountant.

瑪莉：我還有兩個問題。你沒寫到花店的連絡資訊。上次公差旅行的款項（12月17日）你忘了告知會計。

31. 為何男子向另外兩個人說「抱歉」呢？

(A) 因為其他人須替補他的工作

(B) 因為他很抱歉工作表現不好

(C) 因為他的工作一團糟

(D) 因為假期不順利

32. 關於工作細節，下列哪個選項沒提到？

(A) 電匯

(B) 目標顧客

(C) 預約航班

(D) 送花

33. 他為何不能自己做此工作呢？

(A) 他要辭職。

(B) 他要請病假。

(C) 他將去度假。

(D) 他精神狀況不穩。

31.

· 聽到對話，馬上鎖定 **take a vacation**，推測是和「度假」有關。此題屬於細節及推測題，也同時測試考生對慣用語 "take a vacation" 的理解，考生必須先懂這個慣用語的深層意思，再推測哪個選項描述與之有關。考點引用句的另一線索是 do the job，所以 是他希望其他人幫他做工作，當他度假時。(A)選項完整句句意和他要道歉的原因此符合。選項(A)及(B)的是陷阱字，雖然有job和work，「工作」之意，但這兩

句的完整句句意都不符合道歉的原因， 選項(D)尚未發生，因此不選。綜合所述，**答案為(A)**。

32.

· **重點是 work duties，指「工作職責」的意思。**此題屬於細節題，也同時測試考生針對對話中，記得幾個重點，再推測哪個選項描述，是對話中未曾提過的。考點引用句的另一線索字是notes，備註，對話中提過notes的幾點工作，包含電匯、目標顧客、送花等等。因此(A) wire transfer，(B) target customers，(D) sending flowers都是正確，在對話中都曾出現，但並未提過選項(C) booking flight，可推知答案。

33.

· 聽**到對話，馬上鎖定，by himself，自己來。**對話第一句已經破題：I'm taking a vacation from Dec. 15 to Dec 25.，我將於12月15日到12月25日休假，四個選項中，**(C)答案最為符合**。此題屬於細節及推測題，也同時測試考生對慣用語 "by oneself"的理解，考生必須先懂這個慣用語的深層意思，再推測哪個選項描述的意思最接近此慣用語。考點引用句的另一線索字是cover，涵蓋、掩護，對話第一句說明原因：要度假，以及向同事道歉，因為他們必須做他的工作。而這些工作包含幾點，是第二題的考題。題目為can't do himself，不能自己做，因此可得知**答案為(C)**他將去度假。

Unit 12
公司設立日間托孕中心，省下可觀的費用

Instructions

❶ 請播放音檔聽下列對話，並完成試題。 MP3 058

34. What are the speakers discussing?

(A) how much nannies charge

(B) ordering takeout from the basement

(C) hiring nannies

(D) a change in the office building basement

35. What does the woman mean when she says, "Plus, it can save some serious money"?

(A) Brewing coffee by themselves saves lots of money.

(B) The daycare center can save them a lot of money.

(C) Ordering takeout can save a little money.

(D) They need to think seriously about how to save money.

36. Which of the following is closest in meaning to "you win some, you lose some"?

(A) Winning and losing are part of life.

(B) Teaching children about winning and losing is important.

(C) You can't have the cake and eat it, too.

(D) Don't cry over spilt milk.

中譯與聽力原文

Questions 34-36 refer to the following conversation

Mandy: Finally, we're having a daycare center in the office. B1. It can be officially used next month. Really can't wait. Plus, it can save us some serious money. You know how nannies charge these days.

曼蒂： 終於，我們在辦公室要有自己的日間托育中心，在B1。在下個月就能正式使用了。真的等不及了。再者，這可以省筆可觀的錢。你知道這些日子保母都收多少費用就知道了。

Cindy: I've been waiting for this for three years, but with B1 being a daycare center, we won't be having a coffee shop. There's simply no room for a coffee shop.

辛蒂： 我一直期待這個有三年了，但是隨著B1成了日間托育中心，我們就沒有咖啡店了。顯然沒有空間給咖啡店了。

Jack: So, from next month, we have to order a takeout or brew the coffee ourselves. I'm gonna miss those snacks, coffee, hand-made bagels, and tuna sandwiches.

傑克： 所以從下個月，我們必須訂購外食或自己釀咖啡了。我真的會想念那些甜點、咖啡、人工製的貝果和鮪魚三明治。

Cindy: As a saying goes, you win some, you lose some.

辛蒂：有句俗諺說，有得必有失。

選項中譯與解析

34. 談話者正在討論什麼？

(A) 保姆收多少費用

(B) 從地下室點餐

(C) 雇用保姆

(D) 辦公大樓地下室的改建

35. 當女子說「再者，這可以省筆可觀的錢」，其意為何？

(A) 自己煮咖啡可以省很多錢。

(B) 日間托育中心可以替他們省很多錢。

(C) 訂購外食可以省點錢。

(D) 他們需要認真思考如何省錢。

36. 下列選項何者最接近「你贏的同時，也輸掉了些東西」？

(A) 輸贏是生活的一部分。

(B) 教導兒童輸贏的重要性。

(C) 魚與熊掌無法兼得。

(D) 覆水難收。

34.

· 聽到對話，馬上鎖定 **daycare center** 和**B1**，是「日間托育中心」和地下室一頭的意思。此題屬於推測題，對於對話必須理解來龍去脈，再推測哪個選項描述的意思最接近此題目所要的答案。考點引用句的另一線索是no room for a coffee shop，由於第一句說道：要有自己的日

間托育中心，在B1。以及對話中：with B1 being a daycare center，隨著B1成了日間托育中心，因此可知道B1將會改造成托育中心。with 在此是指隨著。

35.

· **聽到對話，馬上鎖定 serious money推測是「～錢」的意思。** 此題屬於推測題，也同時測試考生對慣用語"can save us some serious money"的理解，考生必須先懂這個慣用語的深層意思，再推測哪個選項描述的意思最接近此慣用語。考點引用句的另一線索字是save「省錢」，在第一段對話中，提到托育中心，之後說了一句plus，用意為補充說明。此句為：it can save some serious money. 因此由前後對話，可推知因為托育中心的原故，省下很多錢。serious是嚴肅，嚴重的，**serious money是片語，指一大筆錢。**

36.

· **聽到對話，馬上鎖定，win 和lose 推測是「得失」方面的題目。** 本題答案出現兩句俚語，難度較高。此題屬於推測題，也同時測試考生對慣用語"you win some, you lose some"的理解，考生必須先懂這個慣用語的深層意思，再推測哪個選項描述的意思最接近此慣用語。本句考考生對慣用語的熟悉度。(A) Winning and losing are part of life.，輸贏是生活的一部分。(B) Teaching children about winning and losing is important.，教導兒童輸贏的重要性。winning和losing 是陷阱，讓考生誤以為最接近題意。(C) You can't have the cake and eat it, too.，魚與熊掌無法兼得。接近題目含意。(D) Don't cry over spilt milk.，覆水難收。毫無關係。**考生如果無法理解所有選項描述，仍然有辦法破解，針對談話中， 提到托嬰中心，省很多錢，但是卻沒有咖啡廳的空間等等內容，仍可判斷出答案。**

聽力模擬試題

▶ **PART 3** MP3 059

Directions: In this part, you will listen to several conversations between two or more speakers. These conversations will not be printed and will only be spoken one time. For each conversation, you will be asked to answer three questions. Select the best response and mark the corresponding letter (A), (B), (C), (D) on the answer sheet.

32. Why did the man say, "perhaps... not that close to them"?
(A) Because those monkeys were pushing him
(B) He wanted the others to follow the rule not to get close to the monkeys.
(C) Because he did not want the others to frighten the monkeys
(D) He's trying to persuade the others to stay away from the monkeys.

33. Which of the following is the closest to "agitated"?
(A) excited
(B) disturbed and upset
(C) adorable and sweet
(D) frightened

34. According to the context of the conversation, why did the woman say, "can't we just have some sushi and seafood"?
(A) She heard that sushi and seafood in Arashiyama are delicious.
(B) Arashiyama is famous for sushi and seafood.

(C) She is not interested in seeing monkeys, and would rather do something else.

(D) Seeing those monkeys eating reminds her it's dinner time.

proposal	Budget
A	20 million dollars
B	2 billion dollars
C	20,000,000 dollars

35. Who might these speakers be?
(A) construction workers
(B) bank investors
(C) construction company employees
(D) students studying architecture

36. What is the special situation regarding proposal A?
(A) It did not pass the evaluation by the Department of Environmental Protection
(B) It is being assessed by the Department of Environmental Protection.
(C) The government does not allow construction in that place in proposal A.
(D) Proposal A will cost too much money.

37. What does the woman mean by saying "we haven't reached a consensus..."?
(A) We still need to reach an agreement.
(B) We still need to do more research.
(C) We have reached a conclusion.
(D) We need to carry out more surveys.

Movie	Ratings
A	PG
B	PG-13
C	R
D	G

38. What is the purpose of the conversation?
(A) purchasing the tickets to a movie
(B) deciding who will go see movies
(C) asking for the suggestions about a movie
(D) asking how much the tickets will cost

39. Why does the woman recommend movie B or D?
(A) The content of movie B or D is more appropriate for children.
(B) Movie B and D are both animations.
(C) The tickets to movie B or D are on discount.
(D) Both movie B and D receive high accolades.

40. Why is movie C not recommended?
(A) It has lots of violence.
(B) Some scenes are not proper for children.
(C) The tickets to movie C were sold out.
(D) It received horrible reviews.

Candidates	photo
A	High fashion
B	commercial
C	commercial
D	High fashion

41.What are the speakers talking about?
(A) a catwalk
(B) models' performances
(C) a fashion show
(D) which model is prettier

42.According to the speaker, what is wrong with candidate B?
(A) Her walk is terrible.
(B) Her photos are not stunning.
(C) She has an attitude problem.
(D) She's too short.

43.Which of the following best explains, "her photos are stunning"?
(A) Her photos are breathtakingly beautiful.
(B) Her photos are very shocking.
(C) She does not perform well in photoshoots.
(D) She works well with photographers.

44.What does the man think about the offer?
(A) He is confused.
(B) He is disappointed.
(C) He is very curious.
(D) He is very interested.

45.According to the woman, what are the responsibilities of the spokesperson?
(A) taking campaign photos
(B) shooting commercials for the Medical Center
(C) building a healthy image of the Medical Center
(D) going through a surgery

46.What is the man probably going to do after the conversation?
(A) registering for a surgery

1 新多益基礎對話演練

2 新多益單篇對話和解析

3 新多益對話模擬試題

(B) revising the contract
(C) taking campaign photos
(D) signing the contract

47.What is the problem with the sample?
(A) It is smaller than expected.
(B) It was not produced under the SOP guidelines.
(C) It does not meet the lab standard.
(D) It is contaminated.

48.Which of the following is the closest in meaning to "negligence" as in "it could be negligence on our part"?
(A) not paying enough attention
(B) finishing the production too fast
(C) abiding by the guidelines
(D) not cooperating with FDA

49.What will the speakers probably do after the conversation?
(A) talking to FDA
(B) talking to lab employees
(C) examining the sample again
(D) devising more scrupulous rules

50.How long does the entire trip take?
(A) 10 days
(B) 14 days
(C) A week
(D) 4 days

51.Why does the man say, "there is going to be a really tight deadline"?
(A) because the budget is too short to shoot for a long time
(B) because the story editors speed up to meet the deadline
(C) because the time will be four months shorter

(D) because the film company changes the date

52. Who will not be going to this trip?
    (A) story editors
    (B) the boss
    (C) programmers
    (D) photographers

53. Why does the man say, "I will be needing a doggie bag"?
    (A) He is with a dog.
    (B) He might be having a vomit soon.
    (C) He is allergic with the lobster.
    (D) He wants to wrap the leftovers.

54. How much does the dessert cost?
    (A) It depends.
    (B) It's free.
    (C) It will be deducted from their company credit card.
    (D) It's added benefit if you are using a premium credit card.

55. Which of the following item is not in the doggie bag?
    (A) the lobsters in the bread
    (B) steamed crabs
    (C) ice cream castle
    (D) fired squid

56. What does "eyeing on the house" mean?
    (A) have to take a thorough look at the house
    (B) can't wait to see the house
    (C) have a less keen interest in the house
    (D) have a strong interest in the house

57. What is the purpose of saying "tomorrow I'm swamped with work"?

(A) to show her work is more important than the house
(B) to let the buyer know potential buyers will be the first to see the house
(C) to emphasize she is a conscientious worker
(D) to make the buyer more eager to take a look at the house

58. When will the buyer visit the house?
(A) Friday
(B) next Monday
(C) Wednesday before noon
(D) Thursday before noon

59. What is the purpose of saying "let's not jump right to that"?
(A) because cat got her tongue
(B) because the owner didn't tell her that part
(C) to emphasize she is a shrew negotiator
(D) to procrastinate the house price part and also have some time to show other parts that are fantastic

60. Which of the following is what the buyer finds pleasing to look at?
(A) domestic fowls
(B) squirrels
(C) amphibians
(D) snakes

61. Which of the following is what the buyer dreads?
(A) raccoons
(B) monkeys
(C) frogs
(D) domestic fowls

 62. Why does the woman say, "I guess someone has done her homework"?

(A) to clarify that it's tragic
(B) to make a point that the buyer finishes writing an assignment
(C) to deflect the topic that the two are discussing
(D) To demonstrate that the buyer is prepared and harder to convince

63. Why does the buyer say, "that's an extortion"?
(A) she thinks the price is fairly reasonable
(B) she thinks he is being taken advantage of
(C) she thinks the price is too unreasonable
(D) she cannot think of the tactics at the moment

64. What is the ultimate price for the house?
(A) US 550,00
(B) US 750,000
(C) US 700,000
(D) US 625,000

65. Which of the following will not be used to enhance security?
(A) rigorous SOPs
(B) identity check
(C) surveillance cameras
(D) blood sample

66. What does the woman mean when she says "could be an inside job"?
(A) She really wants to help out by entering inside the door.
(B) She has doubts about how the blood sample getting switched.
(C) She remains doubtful about the investigation.
(D) She treats everyone like a suspect.

67. Who could be the female speaker?
(A) a judge
(B) a defense attorney

(C) a lab researcher
(D) the director

 68. **Why does the speaker say, "that makes things a whole lot easier"?**
(A) because there is a new opening drug store in town
(B) because it doesn't need the prescription
(C) because the traffic is not heavy
(D) because the store has the best painkillers

69. **Which of the following kind of medicine is what the speaker used to take?**
(A) Chinese herbal ointment
(B) tablets of aspirins
(C) capsule-made painkillers
(D) powder-made medicine

70. **Which of the following will be applied to before the speaker heads to the drug store?**
(A) ointment
(B) medicine powder
(C) tablets
(D) the painkiller

模擬試題解析

聽力原文和對話

Question 32-34 refer to the following conversation

Chris: relax... this tour package includes a day at Arashiyama. Plus, everyone visiting Japan would love to see these lovely creatures... as you tour guide... it really is my job to bring you guys here.

Cindy: can't we just have some sushi and seafood? Perhaps some wine. I'm not really a big fan of monkeys... and they seem agitated.

Chris: they... are adorable and sweet, aren't they? Wow... they don't usually act this way... I think they are a bit out of control... perhaps... not that close to them.

Jimmy: Ha... perhaps they think of you are a piece of meat... Tasty... and they are hungry.

Chris: haha... True.

問題32-34，請參考以下對話內容

克里斯：放輕鬆...這個旅遊組合包含在嵐山一天。再者，每個來日本玩的遊客都喜愛看到這些討喜的生物...作為你們的導遊...帶你們來這裡真的是我的工作。

辛蒂：　我們就不能吃些壽司和海產嗎？或是嚐一些酒。我真的不是很喜歡猴子...而且牠們看起來很躁動。

克里斯：牠們...是可愛而且體貼的，對吧？哇...牠們通常不會有這樣的舉動...我認為牠們有點失控了...或許...別這麼靠近他們。

吉米：　哈...或許牠們把你當作一塊肉...可口...而且牠們感到飢餓。

克里斯：哈哈...真的。

試題中譯	
32. Why did the man say, "perhaps... not that close to them"? (A) Because those monkeys were pushing him (B) He wanted the others to follow the rule not to get close to the monkeys. (C) Because he did not want the others to frighten the monkeys **(D) He's trying to persuade the others to stay away from the monkeys.**	32. 為何這位男士說「或許……不要那麼靠近他們」? (A) 因為那些猴子在推他們。 (B) 他想要其他人遵守規則不要靠近猴子。 (C) 因為他不想要其他人嚇到猴子 **(D) 他正試著說服別人遠離猴子。**
33. Which of the following is the closest to "agitated"? (A) excited **(B) disturbed and upset** (C) adorable and sweet (D) frightened	33. 下列何者最接近「躁動的」? (A) 興奮的。 **(B) 看來困擾且不悅的。** (C) 可愛且甜美的。 (D) 害怕的。
34. According to the context of the conversation, why did the woman say, "can't we just have some sushi and seafood"? (A) She heard that sushi and seafood in Arashiyama are delicious. (B) Arashiyama is famous for sushi and seafood. **(C) She is not interested in seeing monkeys, and would rather do something else.** (D) Seeing those monkeys eating reminds her it's dinner time.	34. 根據對話情境,為何那位女士說「我們就不能吃些壽司和海產嗎」? (A) 她聽說嵐山的壽司和海產是美味的。 (B) 嵐山以壽司和海產出名。 **(C) 她對看猴子沒興趣,寧可做別的事。** (D) 看到那些猴子吃東西提醒她晚餐時間到了。

答案：32. D 33. B 34. C

解析

- 第**32**題，使用刪去法，(A) 因為那些猴子在推他們，(B)......遵守規則不要靠近猴子，(C) 因為他不想要其他人嚇到猴子，這些細節都沒提及，**故選 (D)**。
- 第**33**題，根據對話，知道agitated形容猴子，又根據「他們有點失控了」，可判斷agitated是負面意涵的單字，比較四個選項，最有負面意涵的選項是**(B)**。
- 第**34**題，在"can't we just have some sushi and seafood"隨後，女生說：我真的不是很喜歡猴子。換言之，她對猴子沒興趣。**故選(C)**。

聽力原文和對話

Question 35-37 refer to the following conversation

proposal	Budget
A	20 million dollars
B	2 billion dollars
C	20,000,000 dollars

Linda: we should begin today's meeting by discussing the construction sites.

Mary: that's right... we haven't reached a consensus since Dec 12th, 2016.

Jack: B proposal is the most costly, but mansions can be built in two years.

Mary: C proposal takes around 5 years... we can't wait for that long.

Linda: but it's actually the money we can afford.

Jack: how about proposal A?

Linda: the place is still under evaluation by the Department of Environmental Protection.

Mary: we should leave board members to decide... we don't even have a vote.

Linda: let's vote... by raising your hands...

Jack: I'm counting the vote... 15 to B, 12 to C, and 13 to A.

問題35-37，請參考以下對話內容

提案	預算
A	2千萬美元
B	200億美元
C	2千萬美元

琳達：我們應該開始今日的會議以討論建築位址開始。

瑪莉：對的…從2016年12月12日，我們尚未達到共識。

傑克：B提案是花費最貴的，但是豪宅能在兩年內建好。

瑪莉：C提案花費大約五年的時間…我們無法等那麼久。

琳達：但這其實是我們所能負擔的金額。

傑克：那提案A呢？

琳達：那地方還在環境保護部門的評估中。

瑪莉：我們應該要留給董事會成員去決定…我們根本沒有投票權。

琳達：我們開始投票吧…由舉手表示…

傑克：我來數下投票…B提案15票、C提案12票和A提案13票。

試題中譯

35. Who might these speakers be? (A) construction workers (B) bank investors **(C) construction company employees** (D) students studying architecture	35. 這些說話者可能是誰？ (A) 建築工人。 (B) 銀行投資人。 **(C) 建設公司員工。** (D) 建築系學生。
36. What is the special situation regarding proposal A? (A) It did not pass the evaluation by the Department of Environmental Protection **(B) It is being assessed by the Department of Environmental Protection.** (C) The government does not allow construction in that place in proposal A.	36. 企劃A的特殊狀況為何？ (A) 它沒通過環保部門的評量。 **(B) 它正被環保部門評量。** (C) 政府不准許在企劃A的地點建設。 (D) 企劃A會花太多錢。

(D) Proposal A will cost too much money.	
37. What does the woman mean by saying "we haven't reached a consensus..."? **(A) We still need to reach an agreement.** (B) We still need to do more research. (C) We have reached a conclusion. (D) We need to carry out more surveys.	37. 女生説「我們還沒達到共識......」的意思為何？ **(A) 我們仍需要達成同意。** (B) 我們仍需要做更多研究。 (C) 我們已經達成結論。 (D) 我們需要進行更多調查。

答案：35. C 36. B 37. A

解析

- **第35題**，由對話第一句we should begin today's meeting by discussing the construction sites.，得知説話者是在會議中討論建案地點，之後提及三個企劃案，綜合以上線索，最佳選項是**(C)**建設公司員工。

- **第36題**，疑問句how about proposal A?是定位線索，回答是The place is still under evaluation by the Department of Environmental Protection.，Sth. is under evaluation類似講法是Sth. is being assessed，某事正被評量/評估，**故選(B)**。

- **第37題**，此題考與we haven't reached a consensus...大意最接近的選項，關鍵字consensus，共識。換言之是我們還沒同意某事，**故選(A)**我們仍需要達成同意。

聽力原文和對話

Question 38-40 refer to the following conversation

Movie	Ratings
A	PG
B	PG-13
C	R
D	G

Linda: Best Cinema... how can I help you?

Mary: I'd like to book two tickets?

Linda: which movie?

Mary: please hold on a second.

Mary: do they want to go to see the movie as well?

Jack: yep.

Mary: Sorry... my boyfriends' two little sisters would like to see the movie with us... so that means four tickets to be exact.

Linda: In that case, I do recommend you to choose Movie B or D. Movie C contains a lot of nude scenes, and PG films include some violence that is somewhat inappropriate.

Mary: in that case, four tickets for Movie B.

問題38-40，請參考以下對話內容

電影	評制
A	家長指導級
B	家長指導級-13歲
C	限制級
D	普遍級

琳達：倍斯特電影...有什麼我能替您服務的嗎？

瑪莉：我想要訂兩張票。

琳達：哪個電影？

瑪莉：請等一下。

瑪莉：她們也想要去看電影嗎？

傑克：是的。

瑪莉：抱歉…我的男朋友的兩個小妹也想要跟我們一起看電影…所以正好是四張票。

琳達：那樣的話，我想推薦你們看電影B或電影D。電影C有很多裸露的場景，而且家長指導級電影包含一些暴力，有點不太恰當。

瑪莉：那樣的話，電影B四張票。

試題中譯	
38. What is the purpose of the conversation? **(A) purchasing the tickets to a movie** (B) deciding who will go see movies (C) asking for the suggestions about a movie (D) asking how much the tickets will cost	38. 此對話的目的為何？ **(A) 購買電影票。** (B) 決定誰要去看電影。 (C) 詢問關於電影的建議。 (D) 詢問票價多少。
39. Why does the woman recommend movie B or D? **(A) The content of movie B or D is more appropriate for children.** (B) Movie B and D are both animations. (C) The tickets to movie B or D are on discount. (D) Both movie B and D receive high accolades.	39. 為何女士推薦電影B或D？ **(A) 電影B或D的內容比較適合小孩。** (B) 電影B和D都是動畫。 (C) 電影B或D的票有折扣。 (D) 電影B和D都受到高度讚賞。
40. Why is movie C not recommended? (A) It has lots of violence. **(B) Some scenes are not proper for children.** (C) The tickets to movie C were sold out. (D) It received horrible reviews.	40. 電影C為何不被推薦？ (A) 它包含很多暴力。 **(B) 有些場景不適合小孩。** (C) 電影C的票賣完了。 (D) 它的評語很糟糕。

答案：38. A 39. A 40. B

解析

- **第38題**，根據對話開始兩句：Best Cinema... how can I help you? I'd like to book two tickets，得知主題是透過電話訂電影票。
- **第39題**，女生提到有兩位小妹妹會一起去看電影，接著售票員推薦電影 B或D，並提到電影C有裸露和暴力場景。換言之，電影C是不適合兒童的。即電影B或D比較適合兒童。
- **第40題**，根據售票員說的：Movie C contains a lot of nude scenes,... violence... ，許多裸露場景......暴力，推測出電影C是不適合兒童的。

聽力原文和對話

Question 41-43 refer to the following conversation

Candidates	photo
A	High fashion
B	commercial
C	commercial
D	High fashion

Jack: what do you think about four candidates' performance?

Linda: I do love candidate A. She looks great and her photos are stunning.

Ken: what about other candidates?

Linda: I love candidate D, but her walk is terrible.

Linda: I think I'll book candidate A for an ad campaign and schedule candidate C for a catwalk of our swimsuits during Fashion Week.

Ken: What's wrong with candidate B? She is pretty and she has a strong walk.

Linda: she is too cocky and she really needs to work on her personality.

Jack: thanks for your time...

問題41-43，請參考以下對話內容

候選人	照片
A	高端時尚
B	商業廣告
C	商業廣告
D	高端時尚

傑克：你覺得這四位候選人的表現如何呢？

琳達：我真的喜愛候選人A。她看起來很棒而且她的照片很美。

肯： 那其他候選人呢？

琳達：我喜愛候選人D但是她的台步糟透了。

琳達：我認為我會簽候選人A作為廣告活動然後安排候選人C在時尚週期間時替我們的泳裝走台步。

肯： 候選人B有什麼問題嗎？她很漂亮，而且她台步走的很穩健。

琳達：她太自負了而且她真的需要在個性上多作努力。

傑克：謝謝妳的時間。

試題中譯

41. What are the speakers talking about? (A) a catwalk **(B) models' performances** (C) a fashion show (D) which model is prettier	41. 這些說話者在討論什麼？ (A) 伸展台 **(B) 模特兒的表現** (C) 時尚展 (D) 哪個模特兒比較漂亮
42. According to the speaker, what is wrong with candidate B? (A) Her walk is terrible. (B) Her photos are not stunning. **(C) She has an attitude problem.** (D) She's too short.	42. 依照說話者，候選人B的問題是什麼？ (A) 她走路的樣子很糟。 (B) 她的照片不漂亮。 **(C) 她有態度方面的問題。** (D) 她太矮了。
43. Which of the following best describes, "her photos are stunning"?	43. 下列何者最能描繪「她的照片很漂亮」？

(A) Her photos are breathtakingly beautiful. (B) Her photos are very shocking. (C) She does not perform well in photoshoots. (D) She works well with photographers.	(A) 她的照片超級美麗的。 (B) 她的照片讓人驚嚇。 (C) 她在拍照時表現不好。 (D) 她和攝影師合作地不錯。

答案：41. B 42. C 43. A

 解析

- **第41題**，綜合第一句提及的our candidates' performance及對話細節photos，catwalk，the Fashion Week等線索，推測出主題是討論模特兒的表現。
- **第42題**，以candidate B當定位詞，說話者對她的評語是：she is too cocky and she really needs to work on her personality. cocky是厘語的形容詞，意為「傲慢的」，由此可推測candidate B是態度有問題。
- **第43題**，考點句子裡的形容詞stunning意為「極漂亮的」，由此可推測(A) Her photos are breathtakingly beautiful.意思和考點句子最接近。

聽力原文和對話

Question 44-46 refer to the following conversation

Jack: you look handsome... so if you're willing to be the spokesperson for our Medical Center... We'd like to give you a 50% discount on the surgery.

Derek: wow... that's an intriguing offer. With that kind of reduction in costs... I might be able to afford a surgery without getting into debt. So what does your spokesman do? Taking the campaign photos or?

Mary: helping us build a healthy image. Letting others know that a surgery can transform how the world perceives you. Appearance still matters when you go to interviews and dates. People love to be around good-looking people.

Derek: Is this a revised version of the contract... and where do I need to sign?

問題44-46，請參考以下對話內容

傑克： 你看起來英俊…所以如果你願意替我們醫療中心作代言人的話…我們會給你外科手術5折折扣。

德瑞克：哇…這提議真的吸引人。有如此的費用折扣…我可能可以負擔起外科手術費用又不用負債。所以你們的代言人都做些甚麼？替活動拍攝照片嗎？

瑪莉： 幫助我們建立健康的形象。讓其他人知道外科手術可以改變世界是如何看待你的。外表仍在你參加面試或約會時至關重要。人們喜愛周遭環繞著好看的人。

德瑞克：這是修改後的合約版本嗎？…我需要在哪裡簽名呢？

試題中譯

44. What does the man think about the offer? (A) He is confused. (B) He is disappointed. (C) He is very curious. **(D) He is very interested.**	44. 這位男士對提議的看法如何？ (A) 他感覺困惑。 (B) 他感覺失望。 (C) 他很好奇。 **(D) 他很有興趣。**
45. According to the woman, what are the responsibilities of the spokesperson? (A) taking campaign photos (B) shooting commercials for the Medical Center **(C) building a healthy image of the Medical Center** (D) going through a surgery	45. 依照女生，發言人的責任是什麼？ (A) 拍攝活動照片。 (B) 替醫療中心拍廣告。 **(C) 替醫療中心建立健康形象。** (D) 動手術。
46. What is the man probably going to do after the conversation? (A) registering for a surgery (B) revising the contract (C) taking campaign photos **(D) signing the contract**	46. 對話之後男生可能做什麼？ (A) 掛號動手術。 (B) 修改合約。 (C) 拍攝活動照片。 **(D) 簽署合約。**

答案：44. D 45. C 46. D

解析

- 第**44**題，以offer當定位字，男生說：wow... that's an intriguing offer.。intriguing，形容詞，令人著迷的，由此字可推測男生對這項提議很感興趣，**故選(D)** He is very interested.。
- 第**45**題，在男生詢問So what does spokesperson do?之後，女生回答：helping us to build a healthy image，因此**正確選項為(C)** building a healthy image of the Medical Center。
- 第**46**題，此題要考生推測對話之後男生可能做什麼，此題型線索偏向對話快結束時，對話最後男生問：Is this a revised version of the contract... and where do I need to sign?由此可推測接下來的動作是簽署合約。

聽力原文和對話

Question 47-49 refer to the following conversation

Mary: they detected contamination in our sample.

Jack: who?

Cindy: FDA and Department of Health.

Jack: but how? Our lab report shows that all results are within the standard.

Mary: I hate to bring this up... but it could be negligence on our part. Sometimes I don't think they're actually following the SOPs and executing all the procedures as they should've.

Cindy: I think they'll be here in a minute. The press is gonna make a big deal about it.

Jack: I do think we should enforce a stricter guideline for the staff of the product line.

問題47-49，請參考以下對話內容

瑪莉：他們從我們的樣本中察覺到有汙染。

傑克：誰？

辛蒂：食品藥物管理局和衛生部門。

傑克：但是怎麼會？我們的實驗報告顯示所有結果都在標準值內。

瑪莉：我討厭提出這個...但是可能是我們這邊的疏忽。有時候我不認為他們實際上照著SOP程序走，而且執行所有應該要走的程序。

辛蒂：我認為他們可能幾分鐘就會到了。新聞記者又會大做文章了。

47. What is the problem with the sample? (A) It is smaller than expected. (B) It was not produced under the SOP guidelines. (C) It does not meet the lab standard. **(D) It is contaminated.**	47. 樣本的問題是什麼? (A) 比預期的小。 (B) 沒按照SOP準則製造。 (C) 沒達到實驗室標準。 **(D) 被汙染了。**
48. Which of the following is the closest in meaning to "negligence" as in "it could be negligence on our part"? **(A) not paying enough attention** (B) finishing the production too fast (C) abiding by the guidelines (D) not cooperating with FDA	48. 下列何者意思和「可能是我們這邊的疏忽」這句裡「疏忽」的意思最接近? **(A) 沒有給與足夠的注意力。** (B) 產品太快完成。 (C) 遵守規則。 (D) 不和食品藥物管理局合作。
49. What will the speakers probably do after the conversation? (A) talking to FDA (B) talking to lab employees (C) examining the sample again **(D) devising more scrupulous rules**	49. 對話後說話者可能做什麼? (A) 和食品藥物管理局談話。 (B) 和實驗室員工談話。 (C) 再檢查一次樣本。 **(D) 制定更嚴謹的規則。**

答案:47. D 48. A 49. D

解析

- 第**47**題,根據對話第一句: they detected a contamination from our sample.,「他們從我們的樣本中察覺到汙染」,**(D)** 選項:它被汙染了,意思和此句相同。

- **第48題**，此題考negligence的字義，negligence是「疏忽」的名詞。也能從考點句子的下一句: Sometimes I don't think they're actually following the SOPs and execute all the procedures as they should've.，推測negligence是負面意義的字，故**(A)**沒有給與足夠的注意力，是最佳選項。
- **第49題**，根據對話最後一句: I do think we should enforce a stricter guideline for the staff of the product line.，關鍵字是enforce a stricter guideline，**選項(D)** devising more scrupulous rules和enforce a stricter guideline意思相同。

聽力原文和對話

Questions 50-52 refer to the following conversation

Boss: after some deliberation, we've come to a consensus that software programmers and photographers will be going to the African trip... a fortnight trip...

Cindy: I'm a story editor... so I'm always on the list... this announcement clearly has nothing to do with me...

Mark: deep down... I have this odd feeling that it's not going to be that easy...

Boss: ...during this trip... all editors need to focus... the date of the released film is prior to our original date... which will be four months earlier... so there is going to be a really tight deadline...

Mark: ...I knew it... they are not going to spend the money that easy...

Cindy: ...how hard can it be... relax... I already have the concept in mind... this trip is going to be great... traveling... while thinking of something great for the storylines....

問題50-52，請參考以下對話內容

老闆: 在經過一些深思熟慮後，我們已經達成了共識，就是軟體計劃師和攝影師也會參與非洲之旅…為期14天的旅程…。

辛蒂: 我是故事編輯…所以我總會在名單上頭…這個宣告全然跟我毫無關係…。

馬克: 在心底…我有種很怪的感覺是，此趟行程不會這樣的簡單…。

老闆: …在這次的旅行期間…所有的編輯都需要專注…電影上映的日期比我們原先預定的日期更早了…也就是提前了4個月的時程…所以截止日期會是更緊密的…。

馬克：...我就知道...他們不會那麼隨易花這筆錢...。

辛蒂：...能有多難呢？...放鬆些...在心底我已經有了一些概念了...這次的旅程一定會很棒...旅行...而順道構想些棒的題材當作故事情節...。

試題中譯與解析

50. How long does the entire trip take? (A) 10 days (B) **14 days** (C) A week (D) 4 days	50. 整個旅程花費多長的時間呢？ (A) 10 天 (B) **14 天** (C) 一週 (D) 4 天
51. Why does the man say, "there is going to be a really tight deadline"? (A) because the budget is too short to shoot for a long time (B) because the story editors speed up to meet the deadline (C) **because the time will be four months shorter** (D) because the film company changes the date	51. 為什麼男子提到「there is going to be a really tight deadline」？ (A) 因為預算太少而無法拍攝太久 (B) 因為故事編輯們加快速度趕截止日期 (C) **因為時間會比預期的少四個月** (D) 因為電影公司更改了日期
52. Who will not be going to this trip? (A) story editors (B) **the boss** (C) programmers (D) photographers	52. 誰將不會參加此次的旅行呢？ (A) 故事編輯 (B) **老闆** (C) 工程師 (D) 攝影師

答案：50. B 51. C 52. B

解析

· 第50題，這題要掌握的是**fortnight**這個字，代表的是兩週，即14天，故答案為**選項B**。

· 第51題，這題可以定位到老闆講話的部分，所以很明顯答案是**選項C**。

· **第52題**，這題的話要用刪去法，在一開始有講到有兩個職位，原先設定是不同行的，而後來卻更改成同行，還有一點是女子說的story editors的部分，所以只剩選項B了，答案要選**選項B**。

聽力原文和對話

Questions 53-55 refer to the following conversation

Jason: time flies... it's already 3:30 in the afternoon...

Cindy: don't worry... the boss gave us the afternoon off... and I need to go to the lady's room...

Jason: ...OK...

Jason: ...I think I will be needing a doggie bag... too many courses.... and it would be such a waste...

Jason: ...you can wrap up this for me... the lobsters in the bread... steamed crabs

Waiter: no problem... what else do you need...

Jason: ...fried squid also... this tastes really good...

Jason: ...what's this... we didn't order this

Waiter: ...the dessert... it's on the house...

Jason: ...exquisite ice cream castle and a cake... I'm going to take a picture...

Cindy: ...wow a castle... you eat it... I'm feeling a bit too cold.

Waiter: ...how are you gonna pay?

Cindy: ...credit card...

問題53-55，請參考以下對話內容

傑森： 時光飛逝...現在已經是下午3點30分了...。

辛蒂： 別擔心...老闆給我們半天的下午假...然後我需要去下女生化妝室...。

傑森： ...好的...。

傑森： ...我認為我會需要剩菜打包袋...太多道菜了...而且這樣很浪費...。

傑森： ...你可以替我打包這個嗎...龍蝦裏麵包...蒸螃蟹。

服務生：沒問題...還有需要什麼嗎？

傑森： ...還有炸魷魚...品嚐起來滋味相當好...。

傑森： ...這是什麼呢？...我們沒點這個...。

服務生：...甜點...這是餐廳免費贈送的...。

傑森： ...精緻的冰淇淋城堡和蛋糕...我想要拍張照片...。

辛蒂： ...哇！城堡...你吃吧...我感到有點冷。

服務生：...您要如何付費呢？

辛蒂： ...信用卡...。

試題中譯與解析

53. Why does the man say, "I will be needing a doggie bag"? (A) he is with a dog (B) he might be having a vomit soon (C) he is allergic with the lobster (D) **he wants to wrap the leftovers**	53. 為何男子提及「I will be needing a doggie bag」？ (A) 他跟狗狗在一起 (B) 他可能快要吐了 (C) 他對龍蝦過敏 (D) **他想要打包剩菜**
54. How much does the dessert cost? (A) It depends (B) **It's free** (C) It will be deducted from their company credit card (D) It's added benefit if you are using a premium credit card	54. 甜點花費多少錢？ (A) 視情況而定 (B) **這是免費的** (C) 將會由他們公司裡的信用卡扣除消費金額 (D) 這是額外附加的，如果你正使用高級信用卡
55. Which of the following item is not in the doggie bag? (A) the lobsters in the bread (B) steamed crabs	55. 下列哪項沒有包含在打包袋裡？ (A) 龍蝦裏麵包 (B) 清蒸螃蟹 (C) **冰淇淋城堡**

(C) **ice cream castle** (D) fired squid	(D) 炸魷魚

答案：53. D 54. B 55. C

 解析

- **第53題**，男子提到的原因是，食物還剩很多，而食物均高檔，他希望能夠外帶，也有陸續提到想要外帶的項目，故答案為**選項D**。
- **第54題**，這題是詢問甜點的價格，但是在對話中沒有提到食物的價格，也沒有圖表顯示數據，不過可以從服務生口中得知甜點是**on the house**，代表這是餐廳免費贈送的，所以甜點是不需要花到一毛錢的，要選**選項B** it's free。
- **第55題**，這題是詢問項目，可以扣除男子提到的部分，該三項是一定會打包的部分，而對話中無法判別甜點有沒有打包，但既然該三項食品一定會打包代表僅剩甜點的部分，故答案要選**選項C**。

聽力原文和對話

Questions 56-58 refer to the following conversation

Cindy: ...can't believe someone is calling me... wait a second.

Cindy: ...yes... this is she... hmm... what? You would love to take a look of this house... that's fantastic...

Buyer: ...yep the sooner the better... I've been to The King's Lake several times... this would the ideal house for us... just tell us the day... any time

Cindy: ...but... there are also other buyers who are eyeing on the house...

Buyer: ...what?... can we see the house tomorrow?

Cindy: ...tomorrow I'm swamped with work... and the next few days I have agreed to several potential buyers... who have shown a keen interest in the house...

Buyer: ...can you do Friday...?

Cindy: ...Friday... I'm wide open... but the road 555 will be having a construction...

Cindy: ...I guess the quickest date... would be next Monday... if that's ok

Buyer: ...ok... see you on Monday... preferably before noon
Cindy: ...sure... see you then...

問題56-58，請參考以下對話內容

辛蒂：...不敢相信有人來電給我...等我一下...。
辛蒂：...是的...這就是她...恩恩。...什麼？你想要來看下房子...那太棒了...。
買家：...是的越快越好...我曾經去過國王湖幾次...這會是我們理想中的房子了...就跟我們説觀看的日期...任何時候。
辛蒂：...但是...也還有其他買家也看中這間房子...。
買家：可以明天看房嗎？
辛蒂：...明天我的工作排山倒海而來...而且接下來的幾天，我已經同意幾個潛在的買家...他們對房子已經表現得極有興趣...。
買家：你星期五可以嗎...？
辛蒂：...星期五，我相當有空...但是道路555正在修建中...。
辛蒂：...我想最快的日期...可能是下週一...如果這是可以的話。
買家：...ok...星期一見囉...偏好中午之前。
辛蒂：...當然...到時見囉...。

試題中譯與解析	
56. What does "eyeing on the house" mean? (A) have to take a thorough look at the house (B) can't wait to see the house (C) have a less keen interest in the house (D) **have a strong interest in the house**	56.「eyeing on the house」指的是什麼呢？ (A) 必須仔細盤看房子 (B) 等不及要看房子了 (C) 對於房子沒那麼有興致 (D) **對房子有極濃厚的興趣**
57. What is the purpose of saying "tomorrow I'm swamped with work"? (A) to show her work is more important than the house (B) to let the buyer know potential buyers will be the first to see the house	57. 提到「tomorrow I'm swamped with work」的目的是什麼呢？ (A) 顯示她的工作比起房子更為重要 (B) 讓買家知道潛在買家們將會首先觀看房子 (C) 強調她是個認真的工作者 (D) **讓買家更急迫的想要看房**

(C) to emphasize she is a conscientious worker (D) **to make the buyer more eager to take a look at the house**	
58. When will the buyer visit the house? (A) Friday (B) **next Monday** (C) Wednesday before noon (D) Thursday before noon	58. 買家會於何時看房? (A) 星期五 (B) **下週一** (C) 週三中午前 (D) 週四中午前

答案:56. D 57. D 58. B

 解析

・ **第56題**,eyeing on the house代表是看中了,所以也就是選項中的have a strong interest故答案要選**選項D**。

・ **第57題**,說這句話的目的是,其實明明有時間,但是卻裝忙表明很多人要來看房,提高房子價值或讓對方更想要觀看或得到這間房子,所以最可能的選項是**選項D**。

・ **第58題**,這題的話聽力段落有提到最後喬定的看房日期是下週一,且偏好是中午前,所以答案要選**選項B**,另外也要別被noon干擾到而選錯了。

聽力原文和對話

Questions 59-61 refer to the following conversation

Mark: ...I've got to say that you are pretty good at the realtor things?

Cindy: ...thanks... I think they will be here any minutes...

Buyer: ...hi... this place looks terrific... how much does this place cost...?

Cindy: ...let's not jump right to that... this is the owner of the house... and we would like to take you to a short trail... and it heads to the lake...

Buyer: ...wonderful... I thought you are gonna show me the house first.

Cindy: ...this way... besides those domestic fowls... there are some squirrels on the trees

Buyer: ...quite soothing... these swans look beautiful... don't tell me that there are raccoons... they are too playful...

Cindy: ...no raccoons... but there will be some amphibians crawling on the floor..

Buyer: ...the air is quite fresh... and finally... the lake... gorgeous and sanitary... how does this place remain to be a fairy tale-like place...

Cindy: ...some magic perhaps... ha

問題59-61，請參考以下對話內容

馬克： ...我必須要說的是，你真的相當擅長地產銷售的事情？

辛蒂： ...謝謝...我想他們幾分鐘之內就到了...。

買家： ...嗨...這個地方看起來很棒...這個地方要花費多少錢呢...？

辛蒂： ...我們先別跳到那部分...這位是房屋的主人...而我們想要帶你先走下短的小徑...而且小徑是朝向湖泊...。

買家： ...太棒了...我以為你們會先帶我去看房子...。

辛蒂： ...這邊...除此那些家禽類生物之外...還有一些松鼠在樹上。

買家： ...相當撫慰人心...這些天鵝看起來很美麗...別告訴我這裡有浣熊...他們太頑皮了...。

辛蒂： 沒有浣熊...但是這裡有一些兩棲生物爬行在地面上...。

買家： 這裡的空氣相當清新...然後最後...這湖泊...美麗且衛生...這樣的地方怎麼能夠維持的像是仙境一般...。

辛蒂： ...可能是一些魔法吧...哈哈。

試題中譯與解析

59. What is the purpose of saying "let's not jump right to that"?	59. 提到「let's not jump right to that」的目的是什麼？
(A) because cat got her tongue	(A) 因為她說不出話了
(B) because the owner didn't tell her that part	(B) 因為屋主不想告訴她那部分的事情
(C) to emphasize she is a shrew negotiator	(C) 強調她是精銳的協商者
(D) **to procrastinate the house price part and also have some time to show other parts that are fantastic**	(D) **拖延房價的部分並且有時間去顯示其他部分是很棒的**

60. Which of the following is what the buyer finds pleasing to look at? (A) **domestic fowls** (B) squirrels (C) amphibians (D) snakes	60. 下列哪一項是買家覺得賞心悅目的? (A) **家禽** (B) 松鼠 (C) 兩棲類動物 (D) 蛇
61. Which of the following is what the buyer dreads? (A) **raccoons** (B) monkeys (C) frogs (D) domestic fowls	61. 下列哪一項是買家所懼怕的? (A) **浣熊** (B) 猴子 (C) 青蛙 (D) 家禽

答案：59. D 60. A 61. A

- 第**59**題，這句話也是，要對方先別談某個部分，其實有點在拖延或是想要讓對方看看周遭環境或其他對房子有利的所有因素後，最後才來談，有點像談薪水，都理解工作內容等等的在談會比較有利，所以這題要選**選項D**。
- 第**60**題，the buyer finds pleasing to look at可以對應到quite soothing... these swans look beautiful，故答案為**選項A**，swans = **domestic fowls**。
- 第**61**題，what the buyer dreads可以對應到don't tell me that there are raccoons... they are too playful，所以答案為**選項A**。

Questions 62-64 refer to the following conversation

Mark: ...my heart sank... apparently our neighbor told the buyer about a person who committed suicide in the house...

Cindy: ...don't worry about it...

Buyer: ...Actually, I heard about the incident... regarding...

Cindy: ...I guess someone has done her homework... yep it's quite tragic... but... I have got to tell you when he shot himself... he slipped... and fell outside the roof on the road... he didn't die in the house...

Buyer: ...let's get done to business... the price... of the house...

Cindy: ...It's US 750,000... but we have trimmed a little since there was... indeed an incident... so US 700,000...

Buyer: ...that's an extortion... US 550,000 is more reasonable...

Cindy: ...the owner bought the house at a price much higher than that... and with a view like that we'd prefer to sell to the cinema company... which came to haggle with the price with us a few days ago... I guess the price should be 75,000 higher than what you said earlier is that ok?

Buyer: ...fine... let's sign the contract...

問題62-64，請參考以下對話內容

馬克： ...我的心一沉...顯然我的鄰居告訴買家關於一個人在屋內自殺的事情...。

辛蒂： ...別擔心吧...。

買家： 實際上，我聽過這個事件...關於...。

辛蒂： 我想有些人已經事前有做功課了...是的...這是相當悲劇性的...但是...我必須要跟妳說，當他將槍射向自己時...他滑了一跤...然後跌到屋頂後的道路上了...他並沒有死在屋內...。

買家： ...讓我們回到正事吧...房屋的...價格...。

辛蒂： ...75萬美元，但是我們已經減了些零頭...既然...確實...曾經有起事件發生...所以價格是70萬美元...。

買家： ...這真的是勒索...55萬美元才是較為合理的價格...。

辛蒂： ...房屋的主人當初在購買房子時的價格時遠高於這個價格...而且以這樣的景色，我們情願銷售給電影公司...其於幾天前來討價還價...我想價格應該要比起原先你所提的價格再高75000美元，這樣可以嗎？

買家： 好吧...讓我們簽了這合約吧...。

試題中譯與解析	
62. Why does the woman say, "I guess someone has done her homework"? (A) to clarify that it's a tragic (B) to make a point that the buyer finishes writing an assignment (C) to deflect the topic that the two are discussing (D) **to demonstrate that the buyer is prepared and harder to convince**	62. 為什麼女子提到「I guess someone has done her homework」? (A) 澄清這是個悲劇 (B) 強調買家完成撰寫功課 (C) 轉移他們倆人間所討論的話題 (D) **顯示買家有備而來而且更難被說服**
63. Why does the buyer say, "that's an extortion"? (A) she thinks the price is fairly reasonable (B) she thinks he is being taken advantage of (C) **she thinks the price is too unreasonable** (D) she cannot think of the tactics at the moment	63. 為什麼説話者提到「that's an extortion」? (A) 她認為價格相當合理 (B) 她認為他被利用了 (C) **她認為價格過於不合理** (D) 在當下，她想不出任何策略
64. What is the ultimate price for the house? (A) US 550,00 (B) US 750,000 (C) US 700,000 (D) **US 625,000**	64. 最後房子的成交價是多少呢? (A) 550,00 美元 (B) 750,000 美元 (C) 700,000 美元 (D) **625,000美元**
答案：62. D 63. C 64. D	

解析

- **第62題**，買方居然得知了房子的某個消息，所以女子回應了這句話，有點輕描淡寫的帶過，女子是不怕對方得知這個消息會影響到談判籌碼，不過這意謂著比起不知情的情況，買家已經有備而來，是更難說服的，故答案要選**選項D**。

- **第63題**，講這句話有點激動，代表這根本像是勒索，所以很大程度是他認為價格過於高或太過於不合理了，故答案要選**選項C**。

- **第64題**，中間有出現議價的部分，可以綜合下買家講的價格US 550,000 is more reasonable和最後女子提到的I guess the price should be 75,000 higher than what you said earlier is that ok?，故答案為**選項D**，550,000+75,000 = **625000**元。

聽力原文和對話

Questions 65-67 refer to the following conversation

Cindy: Court ruled that the blood sample had been contaminated... so it can't be used as evidence... therefore, I am enacting more stringent SOPs and considering adopting the higher security system...

Mark: What do you mean? You think someone stole the sample and swapped it... so that it can obstruct the justice...

Cindy: it's possible... and could be an inside job... so from now on entering that door requires at least three senior executives' fingerprints on the computer outside the door... and there are gonna be ten surveillance cameras erected in the room...

Mark: ...you totally treat everyone like a criminal...

Cindy: ...it's the company's reputation... and I'm going to hire private detectives to do background checks to see if employees are related to this...

問題65-67，請參考以下對話內容

辛蒂： 法庭判定血液樣本受到汙染...所以這不能用於呈堂的證據...因此，我會制定更嚴格的SOP並且考慮採用較高階的安全防護系統...。

馬克： 你指的是什麼呢？你認為有人竊取了樣本，然後掉包了...這樣一來就能干擾司法嗎？

辛蒂： 這情形是可能發生的…且可能是有內鬼…所以從現在起進入那扇門需要至少三位資深主管的指紋在外頭的那台電腦上感應…而且房間內會裝置10台監視器在裡頭…。

馬克： …你整個把每個人都當成像是罪犯了…。

辛蒂： …這關乎到公司的名聲…而且我打算雇用私家偵探來做背景調查，看看是否公司員工跟這起事件有關聯…。

試題中譯與解析

65. Which of the following will not be used to enhance security? (A) rigorous SOPs (B) identity check (C) surveillance cameras (D) **blood sample**	65. 下列哪一項不會用於提高安全防護？ (A) 嚴格的SOP (B) 身分確認 (C) 監視器 (D) **血液樣本**
66. What does the woman mean when she says "could be an inside job"? (A) she really wants to help out by entering inside the door (B) **she has doubts about how the blood sample getting switched** (C) she remains doubtful about the investigation (D) she treats everyone like a suspect	66. 女性說話者提到「could be an inside job」是什麼意思？ (A) 她真的想要藉由進入內門來幫助整起事件。 (B) **她對於血液樣本被調換的事情感到疑惑。** (C) 她對於整起調查事件抱持存疑的態度。 (D) 她把每個人都當成嫌疑犯。
67. Who could be the female speaker? (A) a judge (B) a defense attorney (C) a lab researcher (D) **the director**	67. 誰可能會是女性說話者？ (A) 法官 (B) 辯護律師 (C) 實驗室的研究人員 (D) **主管**

答案：65. D 66. B 67. D

- 第**65**題，這題是詢問何者不是用於提升安全防護，很明顯答案是血液樣本，故答案要選**選項D**。
- 第**66**題，其實僅是猜測因為血液樣本被換很可能是有內鬼，故答案最可能是**選項B**。
- 第**67**題，這題的話別受到法院等的混淆，女子最有可能是研究中心的高階人員或老闆等，才有可能講出這些話和提升安全防護的手續，故答案要選**選項D**。

聽力原文和對話

Questions 68-70 refer to the following conversation

Linda: I guess I'm having a migraine... Do you still have that aspirin... double dose...?

Cindy: ...let me check... it's not in here... it's not in my drawer... sorry... I'm running out of that pill... perhaps you should go to the pharmacy... Best pharmacy...

Linda: ...yeah... severe headache could kill me... I'm getting my coat and head to the new opening store... by the way do I need the prescription...?

Cindy: ...you're an adult... and drugs like aspirin don't require any prescription...

Linda: ...that makes things a whole lot easier...

Cindy: I used to take the painkillers... they're made of capsules... so no bitter taste... now aspirins are made of tablets

Linda: ...as long as it's not powder kind of medicine... fine with me...

Cindy: before you go... I do have Chinese herbal ointment... you can put some and rub around your forehead... it helps...

Linda: ...thanks...

問題68-70，請參考以下對話內容

琳達： 我想我有些偏頭痛…你還有那個阿斯匹靈…雙倍劑量的…？

辛蒂： 讓我看下…不在這兒…也不在我的抽屜裡…抱歉…我的藥用完了…或許你該去藥局一趟了…倍斯特藥局…。

琳達： …是的…嚴重的頭痛可能會要我的命…我去拿件外套，然後朝新開的店走去…順便一提的是我會需要處方嗎？

辛蒂： …你是成年人了…而且像是阿斯匹靈這樣的藥不需要任何處方…。

琳達： …那樣的話，那麼事情就變得簡單多了。

辛蒂： …過去我曾使用止痛劑…由膠囊所組成的…所以沒有苦的味道…現在阿斯匹靈是由藥錠所組成的。

琳達： …只要不是粉末狀那樣的藥物…我都可以接受的…。

辛蒂： 在你去之前…我確實有中國的草藥藥膏…你可以敷一些並且在你前額周圍擦拭…這有幫助…。

琳達： …謝謝…。

試題中譯與解析

68. Why does the speaker say, "that makes things a whole lot easier"? (A) because there is a new opening drug store in town (B) **because it doesn't need the prescription** (C) because the traffic is not heavy (D) because the store has the best painkillers	68. 為什麼説話者説，「這就讓整件事情容易辦的多了」？ (A) 因為小鎮新開了一間藥局 (B) **因為就不需要藥品處方了** (C) 因為交通沒那麼壅擠 (D) 因為店裡有最佳的止痛劑
69. Which of the following kinds of medicine is what the speaker used to take? (A) Chinese herbal ointment (B) tablets of aspirins (C) **capsule-made painkillers** (D) powder-made medicine	69. 下列哪個種類的藥品是過去説話者所服用的？ (A) 中國的草藥藥膏 (B) 阿斯匹靈藥錠 (C) **膠囊所製成的止痛劑** (D) 粉末製成的藥品

70. Which of the following will be applied to before the speaker heads to the drug store? (A) **ointment** (B) medicine powder (C) tablets (D) the painkiller	70. 下列哪一項可於前往藥局前先行敷用? (A) **藥膏** (B) 醫療粉末 (C) 藥錠 (D) 止痛劑

答案:68. B 69. C 70. A

 解析

· **第68題**,因為不用處方的話就代表事情更簡單了,僅要去藥局講述要購買的藥物名稱即可,所以答案要選**選項B**。

· **第69題**,這題可以定位到I used to take the painkillers... they're made of capsules,所以答案要選**選項C**。

· **第70題**,這題的話很明顯要選藥膏的部分,在前往藥局前友人有提議要她敷上中國草藥藥膏,故答案要選**選項A**。

國家圖書館出版品預行編目(CIP)資料

新制多益聽力題庫：會話大全. 2/
Amanda Chou著. -- 初版. -- 新北市：
倍斯特出版事業有限公司, 2020.12　面；
公分. -- (考用英語系列；28)
ISBN 978-986-98079-8-2(平裝附光碟片)
1.多益測驗

805.1895　　　　　　　　　　109018263

考用英語系列　028

新制多益聽力題庫：會話大全2，附詳盡解析（附MP3）

初　　版　　2020年12月
定　　價　　新台幣420元

作　　者　　Amanda Chou
出　　版　　倍斯特出版事業有限公司
發 行 人　　周瑞德
電　　話　　886-2-8245-6905
傳　　真　　886-2-2245-6398
地　　址　　23558 新北市中和區立業路83巷7號4樓
E - m a i l　　best.books.service@gmail.com
官　　網　　www.bestbookstw.com
總 編 輯　　齊心瑀
特約編輯　　陳韋佑
封面構成　　高鍾琪
內頁構成　　菩薩蠻數位文化有限公司
印　　製　　大亞彩色印刷製版股份有限公司

港澳地區總經銷　　泛華發行代理有限公司
地　　址　　香港新界將軍澳工業邨駿昌街7號2樓
電　　話　　852-2798-2323
傳　　真　　852-3181-3973